VANISHED ECHOES

A Breaking News Story

Luigi Pascal Rondanini

To my dear wife,

You are the most wonderfully grounded daydreamer I have ever known. With you, the whimsical lives side by side with the practical, the fanciful ever intertwining with the sensible.

You taught me that magic is not ethereal but emerges through carrying wonder into the everyday. Our ordinary moments became extraordinary lived with your sparkling mind.

Who else could envision fairy kingdoms while loading the dishwasher, or ponder philosophical truths while folding the laundry? With you, the dazzling lives within the domestic, fantasy flourishing through routine.

While I aimed at the stars, your intuition kept us earthed. My unruly dreams found form through your gentle shaping. Together we built this life dream by dream.

These words cannot encapsulate all you are to me, Maria. May this book stand as a small testament to your singular spirit - at once airy, practical, visionary, and wise. You expanded my small world into one of infinite possibility.

With boundless love and gratitude,

Your husband.

CONTENTS

FOREWORD

The story you are about to read explores a fictional but conceivable scenario sparked by the disappearance of a young girl named Lucy Carver in London.

While dramatised, this account touches on some of Britain's most pressing social issues. The lens of Lucy's disappearance illuminates societal tensions around themes like immigration, inequality, and institutional distrust.

Lucy's tale highlights the power of collective spirit when united behind a worthy cause and its propensity for irrationality when gripped by fear of the unknown. Her journey spotlights the media's role in shaping narratives amidst conflict and crisis.

Originally conceived years ago about some facts that occurred in Rome, this narrative was transposed to a modern London setting to underline the timeless relevance of its core messages around truth, justice and humanity.

Though fictional, the story chillingly evokes dangers that can unfold when social cohesion frays and division overrides reason. It transports you into a conceivable reality where an innocent child's life hangs in the balance, subject to shadowy forces beyond her control.

Above all, this is a story of courage in the face of crisis – of an unwitting young hero and a society seeking to reclaim its principles when they matter most.

I hope you find this dramatised journey through London's darkest autumn thought-provoking. Keep faith that light persists if we dare see it, no matter how lost we may feel. The whole story awaits you.

LPR

1 – UNREST AMID MISSING CHILD

LONDON, 19:35

[Live Breaking News intermission appears on the viewers' screens. A picture of a young girl is behind the speaker]

"Good evening, I'm Tara Jones from London Prime News Network, and before we get to tonight's weather forecast, we want to bring you some breaking news from the Hanwell area of Ealing in west London, near our production centre.

We are just receiving initial reports of a 10-year-old girl, identified as Lucy Carver, who has allegedly been abducted within the last couple of hours. Specific details are still limited at this time, but here is what we know so far:

- Lucy had been attending drama club at the Hanwell Community Centre
- After school today. According to her parents, she left there around 5 PM to walk the short distance home, about half a mile away. However, when Lucy did not arrive home by 7 PM, her parents, David and Elizabeth Carver, called the police to report Lucy missing.

In my communication with Ealing police, they indicated they are in the very early stages of investigating, but the circumstances suggest a likely abduction. Officers only began arriving at the scene about 15 minutes ago and are starting to coordinate a search and rescue operation.

From what we know, police have begun interviewing Lucy's parents and friends from the drama club, looking for any clues on who she might have been seen with or anything suspicious noticed. They also retrieve surveillance footage from nearby shops, transit areas, and stations to see if they capture Lucy walking home or anything unusual.

Additionally, police have released a photo of Lucy, which we have already put up for our viewers. Lucy is described as 4'3" tall with long red hair. She was last seen wearing a black leather jacket, jeans and carrying a blue backpack when she left the Community Centre.

[Bullet points accompany Lucy's picture on the screen]

I'm told police do not have any specific suspects or persons of interest in custody. Their priority is locating Lucy as quickly as possible, given the likelihood she was abducted. They urge anyone who may have seen Lucy, noticed anything suspicious, or have any information to call the tip line immediately.

Our news team has dispatched correspondents to rush to the scene in Hanwell. We hope to have them there shortly to provide live updates. In the meantime, I will continually reach out to Ealing police for additional details we can pass along about the search and investigation.

While we await further developments, I want to reiterate that if you have any knowledge about Lucy Carver's disappearance, please immediately contact the number on your screen. Police are desperate for leads.

This situation is undoubtedly alarming. Our thoughts are with Lucy's family and the Hanwell community this evening. We can only imagine the anguish her parents must be experiencing right now with their daughter's unknown whereabouts or condition.

We appreciate you staying with us on your trusted independent news channel as we carefully follow this breaking story live. The circumstances suggest we could deal with a child abduction here in our London area. We will bring you the latest confirmed details as soon as our news team has them.

As I mentioned, we have correspondents urgently making their way to the scene so we can provide live on-location coverage. I'm checking right now to get an update on their ETA...

[Another broadcaster reads other news]

LONDON, 20:15

[Tara at her desk in the news studio]

I've just received word our correspondent Michelle Gray has arrived at the Hanwell Community Centre. Let's go to Michelle live immediately for an update near where Lucy was last seen. Michelle?"

Tara: " Michelle. Please describe what you see near the Hanwell Community Centre, where Lucy was last spotted around 5 PM before disappearing."

[Live shot of Michelle Gray reporting from outside the Hanwell Community Centre]

Michelle: "Well, Tara, even at this early stage, there is a swarm of police activity. Squad cars, officers canvassing the neighbourhood, and search teams coordinating. They appear to be treating this with the highest urgency.

[Footage of police cars, officers searching the area, search dogs]

I spoke to one of the detectives briefly when I arrived. They are gathering surveillance footage from nearby shops and transit stations that may have captured Lucy's walk home. The working theory is someone seized the opportunity to abduct Lucy along this route."

Tara: "Have police revealed anything about the timeline or their investigation?"

Michelle: "Only a little bit more. Based on interviews with Lucy's parents and drama club friends, she left the Community Centre on foot around 5:00 PM. She would often walk or bike along the trail behind the centre through the woods to get home a half mile away.

When she didn't arrive home by 7:00 PM, the parents called the police. Officers believe she disappeared somewhere along that route between 5:15 and 6:30 PM."

Tara: "And no witnesses have come forward yet who saw anything happen along the way?"

Michelle: "Not yet – but police are canvassing the neighbourhood around the trail and woods to see if anyone may have noticed anything suspicious.

They are also appealing to the public for tips. But no eyewitnesses to a potential abduction yet."

[Aerial map showing Lucy's likely route home through woods]

Tara: "What measures are police taking to find Lucy at this stage?"

Michelle: "Full-scale search operations. They have search teams with dogs combing the woods along Lucy's likely route home in case somebody might have hidden her nearby. Helicopters with floodlights overhead to assist. And all area hospitals are alert in case she might be located and brought in."

[Night footage of police helicopters overhead with searchlights]

Tara: "Michelle, police said Lucy's parents contacted them around 7:00 PM reporting her missing. But she disappeared from the Community Centre around 5:00 PM. Do you know why her parents waited those 2 hours before raising the alarm?"

Michelle: "That's a good question, Tara. I spoke briefly with the lead detective, who said the parents initially assumed Lucy had perhaps stopped somewhere along her normal route home to visit with friends when she didn't arrive on time. But when it was 7:00 PM with no sign of her, they began to worry that something more serious may have happened. According to the detective, waiting a couple hours before reporting a child missing is not necessarily unusual in cases like this."

Tara: "Still, those two hours between 5:00 and 7:00 PM could be crucial in piecing together Lucy's whereabouts and finding her. Police will indeed be investigating what might have transpired during that window. Thank you.

For that update, Michelle. Please continue providing any added information from Hanwell as we follow this breaking story. Thank you, Michelle. Please stay on top of any further information from police and let us know as soon as you have additional updates live from the scene."

[Graphic showing timeline from 5 PM to 7 PM]

Michelle: "You got it, Tara. I'll keep you and the viewers apprised of any developments here in Hanwell."

Tara: "Appreciate it. A major ongoing situation as police work urgently to find 10-year-old Lucy Carver."

Tara: "I've just received some new information from local news agencies with reporters on the ground in Hanwell near the search area. I'll read some of these live updates:

- Police are reviewing surveillance footage from a grocery store one block from the Community Centre that shows Lucy walking alone around 5:20 PM. This confirms she began heading home at that time.
- Search dogs tracked Lucy's scent along the trail to the woods but then lost it, concerning police she may have gotten into a vehicle at that point.
- Police are urging residents to check their properties, garages, sheds, etc., in case Lucy is hidden nearby.

These updates validate the police's theory that Lucy disappeared while walking home from the Community Centre.

Next, let's return to our correspondent, Michelle Gray, who gathers reactions from bystanders near the search area. Michelle, what are people in the community saying?"

[Live shot of Michelle interviewing worried resident]

Michelle: "Tara, there is a mix of reactions from worried residents who have gathered. Some are criticising local government and police for not preventing this. Others blame recent immigrants for the crime. But all are sharing hopes and prayers for Lucy's safe return. Here's one local parent I just spoke with:"

Bystander: "We've always felt Hanwell was a safe neighbourhood until now. My wife and I are horrified, thinking this could have happened to our daughter, who walks the same route. We must find who is responsible and get justice for Lucy and her family."

Michelle: "So a very shaken community grappling with how

something like this could happen in their backyard, Tara. But all shared messages of hope and support for the search."

Tara: "Understandably, a wide range of strong reactions is emerging tonight. Thank you, Michelle. We'll check back for more updates from Hanwell. Time for the commercials."

LONDON, 20:25

Tara: "Let's return to Michelle Gray in Hanwell for the latest developments she's gathering there. Michelle, what are you hearing?"

[Live shot of Michelle Gray reporting from Hanwell]

Michelle: "I have a few new updates, Tara:

[Photo of MP Mark Townsend shown]

[Graphic with text of police statement about combing social media]

- The local MP Mark Townsend just issued a statement saying his thoughts are with Lucy's family and promising constituents this will be thoroughly investigated.
- According to media sources, police have obtained a search warrant and are now combing through Lucy's social media activity for clues.
- I'm also being told that due to the severity of the situation, our TV network will be cancelling all regularly scheduled programming for the rest of the evening to provide continuous coverage and updates on Lucy's disappearance.

So clearly, this story requires the full resources of law enforcement and media without distraction overnight until there is some resolution on finding Lucy and getting to the bottom of this."

Tara: "Absolutely, this is the only story that matters now. Our sole focus is providing the latest information to the public on Lucy. Thank you again, Michelle. Please send any major updates from Hanwell as we keep our coverage going through the night."

Tara:" Michelle, sorry, Michelle, you just mentioned police are combing through Lucy's social media activity for clues. Given her young age, do we know if Lucy even had access to social media or a mobile phone?"

Michelle:" That's an important question, Tara. From what police have said so far, Lucy did have a mobile phone that she would sometimes use to message friends and family. It appears her parents monitored her social media accounts, which investigators are reviewing closely for any signs of suspicious communication."

Tara:" I would imagine most children Lucy's age don't have much if any, social media presence. But as we know, online activity reveals much about who someone might connect with. It is thoughtful of the police to examine her profiles and contacts for any leads thoroughly. Please keep us updated if those efforts yield anything significant."

[Stock image of someone's social media profile/activity]

Michelle:" Will do. The social media angle could provide some clues in a case like this with a young child. I'll pass along any developments from investigators on that front."

Tara: "Before we take a brief break, let's recap what we know as the search continues for 10-year-old Lucy Carver, who disappeared earlier this evening in the Hanwell area of Ealing, west London.

[Photo of Lucy shown]

Lucy was last seen around 5 PM when she left the Hanwell

Community Centre, where she attends an after-school drama club. She was expected to walk the short distance to her home but never arrived, prompting her worried parents to contact police around 7 PM.

[Map graphic tracing Lucy's likely route home]

[Footage of police search efforts shown]

An intensive search operation is now underway, with police combing the area along Lucy's likely route, interviewing friends and family, and reviewing surveillance footage for clues. They also urge anyone with information to call the tip line immediately.

While the circumstances point to a likely abduction, police currently have no suspects in custody but are following all leads and working urgently to find Lucy.

LONDON, 20:40

We are continuing the live coverage of this developing story. But first, let's take a look at the weather forecast across the London area and specifically Hanwell, where the search is centred:

[Weather map graphic showing temperatures across the UK]

[Timelapse footage of search crews with superimposed wind speed and overnight low temperature in Hanwell]

Across England, we are expecting a cold night with lows around freezing and a few flurries possible, especially in northern areas. In London and the surrounding region, expect temperatures to dip down to about 1 degree Celsius overnight.

[Satellite imagery of cloudy skies over London and Hanwell]

We report winds from the northwest at around ten mph. Skies will be clear, allowing complete visibility, which may assist search efforts through the night under floodlights and helicopters.

[Wind arrows on map animation showing light winds from the west]

[View of search crews with superimposed temperature graphic for Hanwell area]

No precipitation is expected, which is welcome news for the extensive police search operations outside. We will see sun in the morning, with highs rebounding to about 8 degrees in London tomorrow.

[Sunrise timelapse for next morning with temperature graphic]

Specifically in the Hanwell neighbourhood where Lucy disappeared, clear and cold later in the night with lows of 1 degree. Winds light from the west up to 11 mph. Visibility is high despite darkness, which aids the search.

Dry conditions continue into tomorrow, with partly sunny skies by afternoon and highs in Hanwell reaching 7 degrees.

[Return to anchor at news desk]

LONDON, 20:43

Tara: "We will have more updates on this developing story in just a few minutes. Please stay with us as we continue our live coverage of the search for Lucy Carver."

[commercials are broadcast]

LONDON 20:47

Tara: "I have some important updates regarding 10-year-old Lucy Carver's disappearance in Hanwell earlier this evening. Our correspondent Michelle Gray has new information from the police – let's go live with Michelle now.

[Footage of white van from surveillance video]

Michelle: "Thanks Tara. Investigators have narrowed Lucy's timeline considerably after reviewing surveillance footage from cameras in the area. There is footage of her leaving the Community Centre at 5:22 PM as she headed home. Then, separate footage that does not show Lucy passing by a grocery store blocks away at 5:33 PM. So, police believe she disappeared between 5:22 and 5:33 PM today."

[Map graphic with timeline pinpointing Lucy's movements]

Tara: "And what does this tell police about how she may have disappeared?"

Michelle: "Well, in that same footage, they spotted a mysterious white van in the area that has become a major focal point. The working theory is that Lucy was abducted and put in this van sometime during those 11 minutes. And the fact it hasn't been seen since means it could be anywhere within a wide radius by now after more than 3 hours."

Tara: "Any information on identifying the van?"

Michelle: "Not yet – it's a common white commercial-style van with no discernible markings. But police are enhancing the footage and looking for small clues to help ID the vehicle."

Tara: "And still no witnesses who may have seen something firsthand have come forward?"

Michelle: "Unfortunately, still none at this point. Though police are desperately hoping someone may provide information soon."

[Photos of police canvassing neighbourhood]

Tara: "The mood there?"

Michelle: "Sombre. More and more people are gathering near the Community Centre and search area, hoping to help or find answers. But this is making it difficult for police and the investigation. Extra officers are being called in from other boroughs to help manage the scene."

Tara: "Clearly a challenging situation as the night goes on. Thank you, Michelle. We'll check back soon for any other updates from Hanwell."

Tara: "I've just received an update from Hanwell police asking all area residents to remain indoors tonight. They report groups of people marching from Southall and Acton towards Hanwell carrying anti-police and anti-government messages after Lucy's disappearance.

[Aerial footage of protestors converging on Hanwell courtesy of the Metropolitan Police]

Additionally, through social media organising, more protesters across London are travelling to Hanwell, including some from right-wing anti-migrant groups. There are also counter-protesters arriving to oppose the right-wing presence.

Police are deeply concerned this will escalate an already tense situation. To help us understand what is happening, I'm joined now by John Morris, our network's political editor, and Ryan Shaw, spokesperson for the right-wing group Protect Britain Now. Thank you both for coming on. John, what do you make of these organised protests converging in Hanwell tonight?"

[Split screen with John Morris in the studio on the left and Hanwell protest footage on the right]

[graphic showing bullet points about Protect Britain Now:

- Far-right anti-immigrant organisation

- Founded in 2016 by Ryan Shaw and Alan Wright

- Based in London with an estimated membership of 15000, but with 250,000 supporting their manifesto and actions

- Opposes multiculturalism, wants stricter immigration controls

- Blames immigrants for economic problems and crime

- Accused of racism and spreading misinformation about minorities

- Has staged frequent demonstrations in communities with high immigrant populations

- Seeks to influence policy by lobbying MPs and disrupting public events

- Known for provocative social media posts and viral videos

- Critics say the group promotes xenophobia and division.]

John: "Well, Tara, this seems to respond to Lucy's disappearance's lack of answers so far. Groups with existing grievances against government and law enforcement are seizing on this case to advance their agendas."

Tara: "And Ryan, what is your group's purpose in Hanwell tonight?"

[Photo of Ryan Shaw, spokesperson for the right-wing group]

Ryan: “We want to defend our community against the migrant threat. This situation has their fingerprints all over it, and we won’t stand by while our children are being snatched from our neighbourhoods!”

Tara: “But what evidence is there this involved migrants when police have no suspects or motive yet?”

Ryan: “Oh come on, they’ll cover it up and say it was just some random drifter. Mark my words, when they find the perp, guaranteed he’ll be a foreign asylum seeker!”

John: “I’d urge caution in assigning blame before we have all the facts.”

Ryan: “The facts are our kids aren’t safe because of these immigrants flooding our borders! The people have had enough!”

Tara: “A highly charged environment is building tonight in Hanwell, it appears. We will keep monitoring the situation closely. Thank you both for weighing in.”

2 – NATION IN TURMOIL

LONDON, 21:00

Michelle: "Tara, I have an important update. Lead investigator Detective Martin Hughes is about to speak to the press here and provide the latest details on the search for Lucy. There is a massive media presence, with our live stream alone being watched by over 4 million viewers worldwide. The comments show huge public interest and disturbing messages of hate and blame."

[Live footage of Detective Hughes at the press conference]

Tara: "Thank you, Michelle. Please send us the feed once Detective Hughes begins speaking so we can carry it live."

[Feed switches to Martin Hughes at the press conference]

Hughes: "Thank you all for coming. I want to express our deepest sympathies to the Carver family during this agonising time. Rest assured, we have all the resources focused on finding Lucy.

The timeline is now clear – she was abducted between 5:22 and

5:33 PM near the Community Centre, and surveillance shows an unidentified white van present. This van has been reported stolen earlier today from a farm in Surrey.

[Photo of the white van from surveillance footage]

There is footage of the van stopping for fuel on the M25 near Chertsey, with the driver appearing to be an Eastern European male in his 20s. We are enhancing images to try to ID him."

[Map graphic showing van's route and sighting on M25]

[Reporters shout questions]

[Enhanced still image of suspect at petrol station]

Hughes: "Please, I cannot provide further details at this stage. I ask the public to remain calm and for any protest groups to please stay home and let us do our job. The mayor's office has also requested groups not converge on Hanwell as it hampers search efforts. We will provide another update when possible. Thank you."

Michelle: "There you have the latest from police – the clearest details yet on the vehicle and potential suspect. But still no word on Lucy's whereabouts or condition. The public anxiously awaits further updates."

Michelle: "Confirming that the suspect appears to be an Eastern European migrant has ignited even stronger reactions here. I'm speaking now with Hanwell resident Thomas Reid, who was at the press briefing."

[Crowd shots with anti-immigrant protest signs]

Michelle: "For all disrupting normalcy tonight, know that your actions do not control our editorial priorities. We report only facts on Lucy as they emerge, ignoring dangerous distractions."

[Split screen back in studio with John Morris reacting]

Thomas: “It’s just as we feared – our government’s reckless policies have let these migrants pour in, and now they’re out kidnapping our children! The police better stop covering for them and get justice for that girl.”

Michelle: “A sentiment we’re hearing from many as foreign involvement stokes additional anger tonight.”

[Feed switches back to studio]

Tara: “Michelle, how will this impact the ongoing police investigation?”

Political Editor John: “It’s extremely unhelpful for the public to jump to conclusions. Police must remain open-minded and follow all leads, not just migrant suspects.”

Michelle: “Absolutely, John. But the fear and suspicion are palpable here, making their job even harder.”

John: “Hopefully, Detective Hughes’ plea for calm will temper some of this vigilantism. Otherwise, the search for Lucy could be derailed.”

Michelle: “Speaking of which, I’m being told protesters are now impacting transit, with several underground lines experiencing disruptions. Police are moving into position to block access to Hanwell itself.”

John: “A precarious scenario unfolding rapidly. Despite all this chaos, we await any update on Lucy’s actual whereabouts.”

Michelle: “I agree. Our broadcast now has 10 million viewers, reflecting the tremendous desperation for answers. I’ll stay beyond my shift with criminal profiler Henry Frost, who’s just arrived. Let’s get his take.”

Henry Frost: "In my experience, sensationalising the suspect often hinders investigations. Police need privacy to follow procedures and evidence. Well-meaning public unrest can inadvertently impede progress."

Michelle: "Wise perspective. But emotions are running high. Do you think police stand a chance at containing this?"

Henry: "It will be difficult, but focusing public empathy on the victim rather than anti-immigrant anger is their best recourse right now."

Michelle: "Sage advice. Thank you for your insights, Henry. A delicate balance for law enforcement on all fronts tonight."

Michelle: "As the night progresses here in Hanwell, the crowds continue to grow despite police barriers and roadblocks. I'm speaking with Paul Cook, organiser of the Protect Britain Now protest group here tonight."

Paul Cook: "We're here to demand action and accountability. The police can't keep the public in the dark while our little girl is missing. And if it turns out to be one of these migrant gangs, there'll be hell to pay."

Michelle: "Strong words from the protesters, who have ignored orders to disperse from the area."

Michelle: "I'm also receiving more updates on the traffic situation. In addition to Broadway and Uxbridge Road being closed off, other sections of the A4020 are now seeing closures and diversions as police try to contain the area around Hanwell itself. But protesters have started marching down side streets, leading to clashes with officers."

Paul Cook: "They'd better not try to kettle us in or restrict our right to protest. The people have had enough of being silenced while these migrants run roughshod over our communities!"

Michelle: "Some heated moments occurred between protesters and riot police. Again, the crowd sizes continue to grow as the night continues. An agitated scene here in Hanwell."

Tara: “Henry Frost is still with us. Based on what we know, can you speculate on what might drive someone to conduct an abduction like this on a random child?”

Henry: “It’s difficult to say definitively without more details. But cases like this often involve individuals with underlying psycho-social disorders and criminal compulsions. The seemingly opportunistic nature suggests a predator acting on twisted impulse.”

Tara: “I’m just receiving an urgent update. Police have identified the suspect seen on the petrol station footage as 26-year-old Nikola Petkov, a Bulgarian national living legally in Britain with no prior record. They are circulating his photo now, asking for any information on his whereabouts.”

[Photo of suspect Nikola Petkov displayed]

Henry: “This new information reinforces my assessment. The lack of known criminal history or connection to the victim points to someone seized by dark urges and fantasies. A dangerous figure who must be caught swiftly.”

Tara: “Very concerning insights. In other troubling news, we are getting reports of riots at the Ealing Broadway Shopping Centre with shops looted and fires set.”

[Shaky video footage from rioting at shopping centre]

Henry: “Unfortunately, not surprising. The volatile mix of fear, anger, and anti-immigrant sentiment boils over easily into violence. Police will have their hands full containing these factors while pursuing the suspect.”

Tara: “A rapidly escalating situation on all fronts, it seems. We appreciate your expertise in helping analyse these developments. A pivotal moment in the hunt for Nikola Petkov tonight.”

LONDON, 21:30

Michelle: "I've just received word from Ealing police that Lucy's parents, David and Elizabeth Carver, will be making a statement from their home shortly pleading for calm during this painful time.

[Photo of Lucy's parents, David and Elizabeth Carver]

[Helicopter footage of sizable crowds and police presence in Hanwell]

Scotland Yard is also dispatching reinforcements to help contain the unrest in West London. In other updates, tomorrow's football match in nearby Brentford has been postponed, and TfL is shutting down all underground stations within a one-mile radius of Hanwell due to the protests and riots."

[Loud explosion is heard, car alarms blaring]

Michelle: "Apologies, we just heard some explosion near here. Perhaps it was a smoke bomb set off by protesters just down the street. The situation is growing very chaotic here. Many angry demonstrators openly clashed with riot police."

[Sounds of alarms and sirens, distant shouts]

[Shot of smoke rising over buildings at a distance as explosion sound is heard]

Michelle: "I need to take cover, but police struggle to maintain control as more severe unrest unfolds. We will keep broadcasting live updates as long as we can safely."

Tara: "Michelle, please stay safe out there amidst the unrest. We've received confirmation that Lucy's parents, David and Elizabeth Carver, will make a live statement from their Hanwell home shortly, pleading for calm. They have requested that you be the journalist to cover their family's message in this painful time.

[Over-the-shoulder shot of parents seated in a living room]

"In other updates, our correspondent in Uxbridge is also reporting open protests in the town centre. And the situation continues escalating severely, with over 20 million people following these events live online on our YouTube channel."

"No statement yet from the Prime Minister, despite the opposition urging the government to address parliament immediately. EU leaders are offering sympathy and asking for protests to stop. The UK-EU bilateral meetings slated for this week have been cancelled."

"Whenever the Carvers are ready to speak, we will broadcast their statement live. Please send us the feed, Michelle and stay safe out there."

Tara: "While we await the live statement from Lucy's parents shortly, let's recap the significant developments in this unfolding situation:

[Graphic showing the timeline of key events so far]

At approximately 5:22-5:33 PM this evening, 10-year-old Lucy Carver was abducted on her walk home from school in Hanwell.

At 7 PM, Lucy's parents, David and Elizabeth Carver, contacted police to report her missing after she did not return home.

Police launched an extensive search operation and investigation, later identifying a mysterious white van present around Lucy's disappearance.

[Surveillance footage of white van]

Surveillance footage tracked the van to a petrol station where the driver was identified as 26-year-old Nikola Petkov, a Bulgarian national living in the UK.

[Photo of suspect Nikola Petkov]

As the night went on, large, organised protest groups converged in Hanwell, stoking unrest, clashes with police, and riots.

The revelation inflamed protester anger and anti-immigrant sentiment; suspect Nikola Petkov is an immigrant.

[Aerial footage of large crowds and police in Hanwell]

Police have been struggling to contain the rapidly escalating situation across Ealing and West London generally.

[Split screen showing chaos in multiple locations]

We now stand at over 20 million people following events online as Lucy's parents prepare to appeal for calm.

An agitated and volatile environment here in London as this tragic event continues unfolding. We will have live coverage of the parents' statement shortly.

It's now 21:47 in London."

LONDON, 22:07

Michelle: "I'm standing outside the Carver home where Lucy's parents are preparing to give a live statement. While we waited, they provided a pre-recorded video showing Lucy's daily route, walking home from the Community Centre. This is in response to criticism questioning why they let her walk alone.

[Shot of Michelle outside the Carver family home]

[Footage from a pre-recorded video showing Lucy's walk]

The video shows a pleasant straight path following a bike trail that cuts through neighbourhood parks. There are quiet residential streets to cross, with calm traffic and good visibility. The route takes about 15 minutes total, walking at a moderate pace.

[Aerial map view tracing Lucy's route]

You can see why the Carvers felt it was safe for independent 10-year-old Lucy to traverse daily. The route stays within residential Hanwell, has other youth and parents commuting, and avoids significant intersections or busy roads.

Hopefully, this provides context as to why Lucy was accustomed to walking this route by herself and why her parents only grew concerned after an unusual delay beyond the expected timeframe. We will be sure to share any further updates the Carvers provide shortly in their announcement."

[Expanded description of the pre-recorded video with superimposed map showing Lucy's typical route home is broadcast]

Michelle: "The video provided by Lucy's parents shows her walk home in detail. It begins at the Hanwell Community Centre, located just off Church Road. After exiting the centre, Lucy proceeds down a tree-lined footpath behind the recreation fields. This peaceful trail crosses over Hanwell train station, where we see a few commuters also walking through.

Lucy then arrives at Hudson Park, a modest community green space she cuts through daily. The trail continues into the quiet residential streets of the Elthorne Park neighbourhood.

At this point, Lucy is seen crossing her first road – Boston Road – using a marked pedestrian crossing with good sightlines. Conversely, she enters Elthorne Park on a paved path popular with local families and dog walkers.

The trail then crosses Fitzhugh Avenue, a modest residential street Lucy traverses carefully. She's now just one block from home, entering the final stretch along Townshend Road.

Soon, she takes one last turn onto her street, Bickley Road. The Carvers reside midway down the block in a redbrick terrace house.

The entire journey appears to take about 15-20 minutes walking at a moderate pace along what the Carvers rightly seem to consider a safe series of trails, parks, and residential streets."

Tara: "I've just received a new bulletin from Downing Street. It states that the Home Secretary is being summoned to Number 10 for an emergency COBRA meeting due to the severity of the unrest unfolding across west London tonight.

[Exterior shot of 10 Downing Street]

[Photo of Home Secretary and Prime Minister]

[Split screen showing unrest and riots in London neighbourhoods]

For our international viewers, COBRA refers to the government's emergency committee that convenes during times of national crisis. Having the Home Secretary called to 10 Downing Street indicates the government is now responding at the highest levels.

[Graphic describing COBRA emergency committee]

The Prime Minister himself has not made any statement, but convening COBRA underscores the grave concern around public safety and the ongoing search for missing Lucy Carver, considering these tensions boiling over.

We will bring you any updates from Downing Street regarding decisions or announcements from the COBRA meeting. But this latest development confirms escalation to the national scale. A tense night across London and the entire nation watches closely."

LONDON, 22:30

Tara: "I have another urgent update to share. We have now received confirmation that the loud explosion heard earlier while Michelle was broadcasting live was a detonation at the Ealing Town Hall building. Despite the late hours, early reports suggest there may be casualties from this blast. We will bring you more details as they emerge.

[Aerial footage showing damage to Ealing Town Hall]

[Emergency vehicles responding to explosion]

This represents a grave escalation amidst the unrest. I want to discuss the implications with our political editor, John Morris. John, what options does the government have to try and regain control of this situation?"

[Photo of political editor John Morris analysing situation]

John: "Well, Tara, convening COBRA is a start, as it will coordinate the national security response. Imposing a curfew is one measure they could take to clear the streets. Calling in the military is more extreme but may be required if local police continue to be overwhelmed."

[Graphic describing government powers like curfews]

[Footage of military forces that could potentially be deployed]

Tara: "What else can be done to ease public outrage fuelling the protests and violence?"

John: "The Prime Minister directly addressing the nation would show leadership. And providing greater transparency on the investigation could go a long way – the lack of information has stoked anger and suspicion."

Tara: "Wise insights on navigating this volatile situation. We'll see what measures arise from the COBRA deliberations. This unrest has become much more than young Lucy's disappearance, touching on broader tensions."

[Montage showing protests, clashes, damage from unrest]

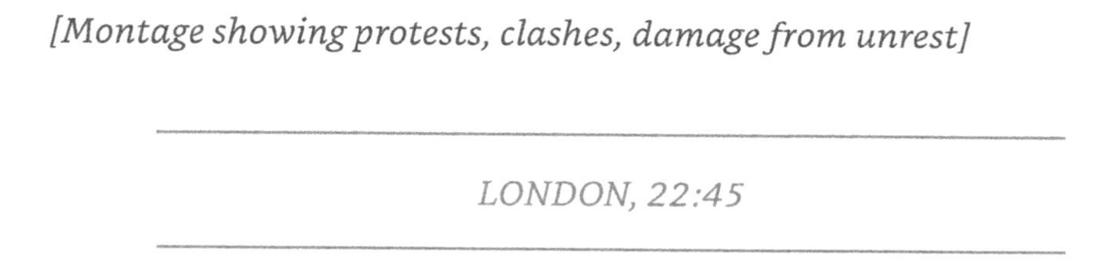

LONDON, 22:45

Michelle: "I'm outside the Carvers family home, where Lucy's parents, David and Elizabeth, are set to make a live appeal. This unassuming redbrick house is where the Carvers have raised their two children – Lucy, age 10, and her brother Michael, 12.

[External shot of the Carvers' house]

The Carvers are lifelong residents of the Ealing community.

[Photo of Lucy with her parents and brother]

David works as a child psychologist at Ealing Hospital, while Elizabeth runs a catering company. By all accounts, they are upstanding local citizens now facing every parent's worst nightmare.

I'm being told all major TV and radio outlets are carrying this exclusive broadcast live at the request of the Carvers.

[Footage showing broadcast playing on devices across the world]

Our viewership has swelled to over 40 million as their message reaches a global scale.

[Graphic showing viewer count at over 40 million]

The comments have been turned off on the live feed due to the flood of abuse and hate posted continuously by viewers. Undoubtedly, this is a worrying sign of the febrile tensions gripping the public during Lucy's ordeal.

In other worrying news, riots have now spread to Margate, where violent anti-immigrant protests are underway. But all attention remains focused here as the Carvers share their pained plea."

[Broadcast switches to the Carvers sitting sombrely]

[Live interior shot of the Carvers seated as they speak, Michelle sitting in front of them]

David: "We cannot find the words to express our anguish right now over our sweet Lucy's disappearance. We feel powerless but must have faith and pull together – not tear each other apart. Our Lucy deserves that."

Elizabeth: [fighting back tears] "Whoever you are that has our baby, please find compassion. We beg you to return her to us unharmed. She must be so scared of being away from those who love her. We want our precious girl back."

David: "Violence and hate will not bring Lucy home. But kindness and community can help see us through this darkness. Stay strong, London, stay hopeful. For Lucy's sake."

Michelle: "That was a heart-wrenching statement from the parents, David and Elizabeth Carver. If I may, I'd like to ask you both to share more about your daughter and who she is. What do you want the public to know about Lucy?"

David: "Lucy is the light of our lives – a bright, joyful girl who loves to sing, dance, and make people smile. She just started the school choir and was so proud. She bursts through the door daily, ready to tell us about her day."

[Home video footage and photos of Lucy singing/dancing/smiling]

Elizabeth: "Oh, Lucy...she is such a happy child, always laughing and giving hugs. I still remember her first steps into my arms. Please, she must be so scared now. We want her home."

[Elizabeth starts crying]

[More cheerful home footage/photos of Lucy]

Michelle: "And your message to Lucy if she can hear this?"

David: *[tearing up]* "Lucy, be brave, sweetheart. We love you so much, and we're going to find you. Think of all our happy memories and know we'll make new ones soon."

[Lucy's brother Michael joins]

Michael: "Lucy, I'm sorry I didn't walk home with you. I should've been there to protect you. You're the best little sister ever. We all miss you so much!"

[Photo of Lucy with her brother Michael]

Michelle: "A family's immense pain and hope laid bare. We thank you for your courage in sharing Lucy with the world. Know that countless people now feel invested in reuniting her with you."

Tara: "Some emails are coming in telling us that it's unclear whether Lucy was attending drama or choir classes. Frankly, it's irrelevant, and whichever is the truth, there's no doubt that the parents are in pain, and this doesn't mean that the Carvers don't even know what their daughter does at the Community Centre."

Tara:" Sorry, I need a break..."

LONDON, 23:00

John: "We will take a short break as Tara composes herself after that emotional appeal from the Carver family. In the meantime, I have some critical updates:

[Shuffles papers nervously]

- Regarding the explosion at Ealing Town Hall, we have the sad confirmation that one cleaner, possibly an immigrant, was killed by the blast, and several others were injured.
- The COBRA emergency meeting is now underway

at 10 Downing Street to address the deteriorating security situation.

- A curfew has been imposed in Margate after violence and rioting
- In London, traffic is gridlocked, with main routes into Ealing now closed off.
- In Acton, police have barricaded and tear-gassed a protest march of around 3,000 people, with clashes ongoing.
- The fires have been contained, but the town hall and a major supermarket on the High Street have suffered severe damage.
- There have been 52 arrests in Ealing as police struggle to restrain the unrest.

It's a dire scenario, the one unfolding rapidly across London tonight. We will keep bringing you the latest developments as authorities scramble to respond. Stay with us for continuing coverage as we await the outcome of the COBRA meeting and any new information on missing Lucy Carver."

LONDON 23:12

Tara: "I'm back now; thank you, John, for covering. I don't mind saying I was pretty emotional after hearing directly from Lucy's family; what they are going through is heartbreaking and frankly upsetting that the public discourse has shifted to violent protests rather than focusing on finding their daughter.

[Photo of Lucy with her family]

But I have some potentially promising news – our correspondent Michelle is reporting on a significant development..."

Michelle: "I've just learned from a police source here that the van driven by suspect Nikola Petkov has been spotted travelling northbound on the M1 past Milton Keynes. West Midlands police are now working to block the motorway and intercept the vehicle at any exit points.

[Map graphic showing van's reported location on M1]

[Photo of suspect Nikola Petkov]

While this sighting remains unconfirmed, it has raised hopes amongst the crowd that an arrest could be imminent. Our sister radio network, MN Radio, in Birmingham, is dispatching reporters toward the police activity on the M1 to provide live coverage."

Tara: "Thank you, Michelle. If accurate, this would be a huge break in the case that could finally end the ongoing nightmare for the Carver family. Our team in Birmingham will have the latest, but this is the first positive development amidst the darkness and violence besieging London tonight. Let's remain cautiously hopeful as police close in on the suspect."

Tara: "This potential sighting of suspect Nikola Petkov's van on the M1 represents the strongest lead in the hunt for Lucy Carver's kidnapper. Our correspondent Michelle first reported the initial tip from a police source in Ealing. Let's get more from Michelle on exactly what investigators revealed."

[Graphic recap of critical details on white van]

Michelle: "Thanks Tara. My police contact here says a motorist contacted emergency services around 15 minutes ago after spotting a white van matching the description of Petkov's vehicle travelling north near the Milton Keynes/Bedford junction. The tipster provided the plate number, which was checked against the APB.

[Animation showing van's reported movements on map]

Dispatch then relayed this immediately to West Midlands police, who sprang into action to intercept the van. They have teams converging on the M1 and side roads to box the vehicle in as it heads northbound away from London. A helicopter has also been deployed to track it from above."

Tara: "No confirmation yet that Petkov is driving the van, but police are taking this credible sighting very seriously. Do we have more details on exactly how they are trying to stop and apprehend the vehicle?"

Michelle: "We're being told traffic units are speeding ahead to set up rolling roadblocks on the motorway to slow traffic and isolate the van. Once pinpointing the location, they will form a perimeter while tactical response officers move in. They aim to establish verbal contact and attempt to take the driver into custody safely."

[Highway footage showing police roadblocks and operations]

Tara: "And what contingencies are in place if the driver refuses to comply?"

Michelle: "From what I've gathered, they are prepared to employ stop strips to disable the vehicle if needed. Beyond that, given the likely presence of Lucy, they will exercise maximum caution – but the clear objective is apprehending Petkov regardless of circumstances to end this ordeal finally."

[Stock footage demonstrating police use of stop strips]

Tara: "The entire nation awaits news of whether this operation succeeds in that goal. Our Birmingham team is en route, and we will cut to them when they are on the scene. This could be the pivotal moment in resolving this tragic situation."

[Live footage from Birmingham correspondent speeding toward the M1]

LONDON/M1 JUNCTION, 23:31

Tara: "I'm going live now to our journalist Rajesh Patel in Birmingham posted at the Coventry junction of the M1, where suspect Nikolai Petkov is due to reach in minutes. What's the latest situation there?"

[Split screen with Rajesh reporting live from the M1 and aerial map view]

Rajesh: "The M1 here is completely blocked northbound, so there's no way for Petkov to exit the motorway. Helicopters overhead ensure he doesn't abandon the van and flee on foot. Police have sighted his van approaching, and armed officers are waiting to intercept."

[Footage of police roadblocks on M1]

[Helicopter view tracking white van]

Tara: "Can you describe the mood there as police prepare to confront Petkov?"

Rajesh: "It's unreal – tranquil and tense. Armed police point weapons at the motorway exit while armoured vehicles block the road."

[Police with weapons drawn at exit ramp]

[Police armoured vehicles forming blockade]

Tara: "What's happening in Birmingham and Coventry?"

Rajesh: "We're getting reports of riots escalating in both city centres and some Molotov launched at a mosque in Coventry. But no casualties have been reported so far. There are also some peaceful pro-immigrant protests occurring that police are monitoring."

Tara: "Any signs of curfews or emergency measures being implemented?"

Rajesh: "Not yet that we know of, but the worsening situation could change that."

Tara: "The podium is now outside Number 10. Prime Minister Chelmsford will soon make a statement.

[Exterior of 10 Downing Street with lectern]

We're also told Buckingham Palace has released one message to the Carver family and another appealing for rioters to disperse."

Tara: "Social networks are inflamed, with the Prime Minister requesting Social Media Companies block hateful messages – so far without response."

Tara: "The UK press remains divided on the protests and violence. The entire Tube network is closed here in London, with more rioting reported in central areas and Oxford Street."

[Montage of conflicting newspaper headlines]

Tara: "With police resources stretched thin, the Defence Secretary has ordered military support be deployed."

Tara: "I want to share some of the headlines we're seeing from national online papers reflecting the divided perspectives:

- The Guardian's website leads with: 'Vigilantes Take to Streets After Girl's Abduction.
- The Telegraph has: "Nation Splits Amid Chaos and Unrest.'
- The Independent's headline reads: 'Where is Justice for Lucy Carver?'
- The Daily Mail's front page announces: 'Mob Rule Engulfs London.'
- And The Sun is going for: 'Hunt for Lucy — Immigrant Sicko Snatches Girl, 10'".

Tara: "A picture depicting a country divided over the origins and appropriate response to this disastrous state of affairs. But all united in the desire that young Lucy is found safe amidst the turmoil."

Tara: "We want to re-centre the narrative on the search for young Lucy Carver, as some unrest threatens to distract from what truly matters most – locating this missing child."

[Photo of Lucy Carver]

3 – SUSPECT UPDATE

LONDON 23:47

Tara: "We have some startling new information about suspect Nikola Petkov.

[Photo of Nikola Petkov]

Police have raided his home and found nothing indicating he had planned or could conduct a kidnapping. He has no social media presence or smartphone. Our correspondent spoke to his neighbours and coworkers, who expressed shock and praised Petkov as likeable and hardworking."

"Let's bring in criminal profiler Henry Frost, who has joined me in the studio, to make sense of this development.

[Split screen with Tara and Henry Frost in studio and images from the M1 junction]

Henry, how do you explain the contradictions with Petkov's alleged actions? But first, let's get some reactions from people who know him, courtesy of Channel 4 news."

Neighbour: "I'm in total shock. Nikola was the most kind-hearted man, always willing to help neighbours and look after stray animals. I can't fathom him harming anyone, let alone a child."

[Generic footage of Petkov helping neighbour]

Coworker: "Nikola was one of our best construction workers – dependable, diligent, pleasant to be around. You couldn't find a man with more integrity. I can't believe he was capable of this."

[Footage of construction site]

Henry: "This is quite surprising given the assumed profile of the abductor. By all accounts, Petkov does not fit the typical pattern of a predatory kidnapper. No digital footprint or warning signs whatsoever. And well-liked by those who know him. I cannot reconcile these revelations with him wilfully snatching a child in broad daylight."

Tara: "What do you infer from the stark contrast between Petkov's background and the alleged crime?"

Henry: "It leads me to believe one of two possibilities.

[Split screen showing Henry Frost and footage of Petkov]

Either Petkov is a masterfully ingenious predator who has pulled off the perfect deception of everyone around him. Or, perhaps less likely, there has been a genuine mistake of identity, and Petkov himself is an unwitting pawn in this abduction."

Tara: "Incredibly unsettling implications if the wrong man has been pursued. We look forward to further information to resolve these contradictions. Thank you, Henry, for your analysis."

LONDON/M11 JUNCTION, 23:53

Rajesh: "Apologies for interrupting. However, the suspect vehicle arrived on the M1 near the Coventry junction, where police have set up a blockade. This seems to be the pivotal moment in the hunt for Nikola Petkov.

The white van approaches slowly, with a helicopter shining its spotlight overhead.

[Aerial footage tracking van's approach]

Officers have their guns trained steadily as the van creeps to a halt about 50 yards from the exit.

[Police taking positions with weapons aimed at van]

Police in tactical gear have surrounded the vehicle, yelling at the driver to get out with his hands up.

No movement yet from inside the van as police continue blaring orders over megaphones. A tense standoff is now underway as officers close in with weapons drawn. An armoured vehicle moves to block any potential escape if the driver attempts to flee or ram through the blockade.

[Police armoured vehicle pulling across the road]

This situation is delicate, with young Lucy Carver likely inside the van.

Police do not want to spook the driver into any reckless actions. Their aim is de-escalating and apprehending him as peacefully as possible.

The van's driver-side door is opening cautiously. Officers shout for the suspect to lie face down, hands behind his back.

[Door opening slowly, driver emerging carefully]

He complies slowly and emerges from the vehicle. Police swarm to restrain him.

The suspect is now fully prone on the ground, surrounded by at least 20 armed police.

[Suspect on ground, police surrounding him in tactical gear]

He is not resisting as they place him in handcuffs. After securing the suspect, officers are now advancing toward the stationary van. They appear to be opening the rear doors – conducting a rapid search for any passengers inside.

[Officers open and enter the back of the van]

There is no confirmation yet if Lucy Carver has been located. Police remain entirely tactical with guns drawn as they inspect the van's interior.

Stand by – officers are emerging from the back of the van. From their body language, it does not seem Lucy is inside. They confer with each other, looking concerned – likely realizing they do not have the kidnapped girl.

Meanwhile, the suspect remains prone on the ground in handcuffs, remaining compliant. This was not a high-risk armed confrontation.

The driver offered no resistance once police surrounded the vehicle and ordered him out.

But the question now – where is Lucy Carver if not being held by this suspect?

[Officers conferring with concerned expressions]

Officers around the van seem urgently in discussion, reviewing options after apparently not finding Lucy present as hoped.

The helicopter continues circling overhead, lighting up the entire interchange, which remains closed in all directions. More police vehicles, including forensic units, are arriving to process the van for any evidence.

The handcuffed suspect is now being led to a squad car – again showing no resistance. He seems confused or shocked, lacking any volatile behaviours often exhibited by cornered kidnappers.

As the suspect is driven from the scene under police guard, forensics teams inspect the van in detail – photographing the exterior and interior and searching for fingerprints or DNA material.

The mood here has shifted from tense apprehension during the standoff to a more urgent focus on gathering evidence now that Lucy is disappointingly not at the location. Officers desperately hope they may uncover a clue pointing to her unknown whereabouts.

This, fortunately, culminated without violence, but the outcome has raised dire new fears for Lucy's safety if she was not being held by this long-sought suspect after all. It was a potentially devastating setback, but police exhaustively pursued every lead.

That wraps up this pivotal sequence of events along the M1 tonight. A suspect is now in custody, but tragically, there is still no resolution on finding the missing Lucy Carver after hours of torment for her family and the nation. Back to you in the studio."

Tara: "Given the lack of Lucy Carver's presence in the van, it's reasonable to question whether the right suspect was pursued. Henry, what's your take on that possibility?"

[Split screen with Henry Frost analysing]

Henry: "I would certainly re-evaluate the prior certainty around this individual. The profile never quite fit – this outcome further doubts whether police were misdirected."

Tara: "Michelle is in Hanwell getting reactions. Michelle?"

[Feed on Michelle while the images from the M1 continue to flow]

Michelle: "As you can imagine, mixed reactions here. Some believe this proves the suspect was innocent all along. Others are doubling down on anti-immigrant rhetoric despite the setback."

Hanwell Resident 1: "This immigrant man was put through hell just for being foreign. Where's the unquestionable evidence against him? It seems people just saw what they wanted."

[Shot of Hanwell Resident 1 speaking]

Hanwell Resident 2: "So we're back to square one even though they said they had the guy dead to rights? It's these migrants causing chaos!"

[Shot of Hanwell Resident 2 speaking]

LONDON, 00:18

Tara: "A divided public processing this turn of events. Meanwhile, the Prime Minister is now delivering an address."

[Split screen showing PM address and various crowd reactions]

PM Chelmsford: "A curfew is being imposed from midnight until 8 AM in Ealing and surrounding boroughs. The suspect apprehended tonight remains innocent until proven guilty. The government has a firm grip on immigration, so politicising this case is unnecessary. Military personnel are being deployed to support police in maintaining order."

Tara: "It's approaching 00:20 AM after nearly 5 hours covering these fast-moving developments. Let's take a short break to process this dramatic reversal in seeking answers."

[Brief break graphic]

Prime Minister: "I want to express my deepest sympathies tonight to Lucy Carver's family, friends, and the Hanwell community. Know that my government will follow events closely and do everything we can to help bring Lucy home and the perpetrator to justice..."

[Full PM statement is scrolling on the screen]

Tara: "As we await further updates, let's recap what's transpired tonight in the search for 10-year-old Lucy Carver, who went missing earlier this evening.

[Graphic showing the timeline of key events so far]

[Police highway standoff]

- Lucy was abducted between 5:22 PM and 5:33 PM while walking home from school in Hanwell.
- An extensive police search and investigation was launched

to find her.

- Around 9 PM, a suspect was identified based on surveillance footage – 26-year-old Nikola Petkov.
- Petkov's white van was tracked heading north and intercepted by police at Junction 17 of the M1.
-

[Surveillance footage of white van]

- In a dramatic highway standoff, Petkov was apprehended without incident.
- However, a search of his van did not locate Lucy, leaving police unsure If they had the right suspect.
- This sparked confusion and mixed reactions from both the public and the police.
- The Prime Minister addressed the nation, declaring a curfew in Ealing and offering sympathy to Lucy's family.
- But nearly 7 hours after her disappearance, Lucy's whereabouts remain unknown, leaving the entire country distraught but hoping for her safe return.

[Photo of Lucy Carver]

This is a brief recap of the critical events that have unfolded over tonight's breaking news coverage as the active search for answers in Lucy Carver's abduction continues. Stay with us."

[Breaking News Bulletin]

Lorna: "Good evening, I'm Lorna Archer, reporting from London.

Headlines tonight:

- Curfew Imposed in Multiple Boroughs: The Prime Minister announces a curfew until 8 AM in the boroughs of Ealing, Hounslow, Hillingdon, and Brent. Curfews are also being enacted in other English cities on a local basis.

-

[Overlay graphic highlighting curfew areas]

[Damage footage from unrest]

- Ealing is currently cordoned off, with no roads open for entry, as authorities work to restore order and ensure public safety following recent unrest.

-

[Empty train platforms]

- All TfL services shut until 9 AM due to operational repositioning after last night's events. Delays are likely as abandoned trains are cleared from stations.
- Tragic news from Ealing as one person has died, and others are hospitalised following a bomb explosion. Authorities are actively investigating the incident.
- Across London, 450 arrests have been made in connection to the riots that erupted following the kidnapping of Lucy Carver. Police maintain efforts to restore order and ensure public safety.
- Citizens are entreated to adhere to curfew orders and stay informed about transit updates. As the situation continues unfolding, it's vital to prioritise safety and cooperation with the government.

That concludes this update. Stay tuned for further developments on the evolving situation. I'm Lorna Archer, reporting from London. Back to you."

Tara: "Thank you, Lorna. We're returning to our live breaking news coverage as the search continues for 10-year-old Lucy Carver, who went missing in Hanwell yesterday evening.

While a suspect was apprehended overnight, police confirmed that Lucy was not in his van, leaving her unknown whereabouts.

Officers are actively pursuing new leads and have reopened the investigation.

I want to go now to our correspondent Michelle Gray, live in Hanwell, where Lucy disappeared and the search is centred. Michelle, what's the latest from the police?"

[Split screen with Tara in the studio and Michelle on scene]

Michelle: "Thank you, Tara. Authorities are back to square one after the disappointing developments with the suspect last night. But they're wasting no time ramping up operations tonight here in Hanwell..."

LONDON/BIRMINGHAM, 00:47

Tara: "I'm advised a renewed investigative focus has been formed primarily to re-canvass the area where Lucy disappeared.

[Footage of police re-canvassing Hanwell neighbourhood]

They are re-interviewing residents along her walk-home route and combing that vicinity for any evidence previously overlooked.

Additionally, digital forensics teams dig deeper into Lucy's online activity and contacts. All CCTV footage is being reviewed again frame-by-frame for any possible leads.

Beyond the investigation itself, police have over one hundred officers patrolling Ealing today to discourage any resumption of unrest. So far, the curfew has contained things, but tensions remain high."

Tara: "While tensions may boil over in the streets, our small local station remains focused on providing updates about Lucy. The protests cannot obscure our journalistic duty surrounding her disappearance."

Tara: "And what's the mood like in Hanwell, Michelle?"

Michelle: "A mix of frustration and hope. People want answers, but they are also energised to help find Lucy. There's a sense of community again rather than the anger we saw tonight."

[Crowd shots in Hanwell showing concerned but hopeful people]

Tara: "Thank you for that update from Hanwell. A renewed sense of urgency within the ranks."

Tara: "We go back to our correspondent Rajesh Patel in Birmingham with the latest on the apprehended suspect there.

[Split screen with Rajesh Patel reporting from Birmingham]

Rajesh, have police revealed anything more about his connection to Lucy's disappearance?"

Rajesh: "They are still being tight-lipped about him, only confirming he is still in custody but not formally charged yet. It seems they initially jumped to conclusions about his guilt yesterday before thoroughly vetting him or his alibi.

The priority is starting fresh to uncover what happened during that brief window when Lucy disappeared. Wherever she is, police vow not to stop until she's located."

Tara: "Thank you, Rajesh. A frustrating lack of answers, but hopefully renewed determination to find Lucy.

[Photo of Lucy Carver]

Please call back if you have a police representative there who can answer some pressing questions, including why Petkov was using a stolen vehicle and how he became a suspect in the first place, given the inconsistencies."

[Shots of Rajesh]

Rajesh: "You're right, those are key questions needing answers. Unfortunately, no one from the police is available here for comment, but I will pose those queries to investigators as soon as possible."

Tara: "Appreciate you staying on top of that. In the meantime, Michelle, do you have any updates on the casualties from the explosion in Ealing and the overall damage to the city?"

[Michelle back on air]

Michelle: "Regarding the deceased victim, police have not released their identity yet as the family is still being notified. But I'm told there were also a handful of severe injuries from the blast.

As for the broader impact, massive damage has been reported across several London neighbourhoods. Fires and looting caused severe destruction in Brixton, Tottenham, Oxford Street, and the Ealing shopping centre. Plus, clashes with police led to hundreds of arrests."

[Montage of footage showing damage from riots/looting]

Tara: "A heavy toll on the city from the unrest tonight. Thank you both for the latest updates. There are still more questions than answers, but let's remain hopeful Lucy can be located safely as the investigation enters this new phase.

As demonstrations rage nearby, we refrain from extensive coverage of the clashes. We will continue training our lens where it belongs – on any developments related to missing Lucy, not those trying to exploit her case."

LONDON, 01:33

Tara: "I have an important update regarding the suspect's van that police had indicated was stolen.

[File footage of white van]

Banstead police have now issued a correction – the van was taken by the owner's son, who then lent it to Petkov to travel to a football match in Manchester.

[Map showing Banstead location]

[Graphic showing van's actual usage]

The son failed to properly notify his father of this arrangement, leading to the mistaken stolen vehicle report. The father informed the police of the misunderstanding before Lucy's abduction occurred.

This grave error unfairly implicated Petkov and wasted precious investigative resources.

[Photo of suspect Nikola Petkov]

[Footage of police search efforts]

The police certainly have some fundamental questions about their false assumptions about the van being stolen.

A miserable series of events brought disaster upon Petkov and derailed the investigation at a critical time when speed was of the essence.

[Montage showing investigation timeline and police pursuing the wrong suspect]

The police were following the wrong trail and lead, squandering valuable time and effort that could have helped drive answers and a safe return of Lucy.

This correction from Banstead police makes it abundantly clear Petkov was wrongly accused.

[Split screen with Tara reporting and graphic "Petkov Wrongly Accused"]

Our hearts go out to him and Lucy's family as we all hope police can still get to the bottom of this nightmare."

Tara: "We're going live to a press conference with London Police Commissioner Chief Ana Martinez, who will address the latest developments in the search for Lucy Carver."

[Live footage of police press conference]

Chief Martinez: "Thank you for coming. I want to make clear that the person of interest apprehended last night, Mr Petkov, has been fully cleared of any suspicion or wrongdoing in Lucy Carver's disappearance.

[Photo of Nikola Petkov displayed behind podium]

The police made regrettable mistakes in prematurely targeting him, and I sincerely apologise for putting an innocent man through such an ordeal.

Despite this distraction, we never stopped pursuing all investigative leads.

Our forces are strained but actively continuing the search for Lucy. And while the curfew has helped, we're still dealing with some unrest and looting across parts of the city."

Tara: "Chief Martinez, how could such a major mistake have been made in falsely accusing Petkov?"

[Split screen showing Tara questioning Chief Martinez at the press conference]

Chief: "We acted too quickly based primarily on incomplete vehicle information. Proper vetting procedures were not followed. It was unacceptable, and we will implement procedural changes to prevent this from recurring."

Journalist 1: "What is your response to claims the immigrant background of the suspect impacted police objectivity?"

[Footage of journalists at the press conference]

Chief: "I can firmly deny any bias affected our judgement. This was an operational failure, not a reflection of prejudices.

[Chief Martinez responding firmly at podium]

We are committed to running a transparent, just police force."

"Journalist 2: "Your officers injured some protesters last night. Could restraint have been exercised?"

[Footage of journalists at the press conference]

Chief: "Regrettably, force is sometimes required as events escalate rapidly. But we strive to de-escalate whenever possible. The safety of all Londoners remains our priority."

[Feed back to the studio]

Tara: "Thanks to Chief Martinez. Still questions about police conduct, but hopefully lessons being learned as the search continues."

4 – UNVEILING SHADOWS

LONDON, 03:15

Tara: "With the focus shifting back to Lucy's hometown of Hanwell, police are going door to door interviewing families, friends, and neighbours who may have any information about her disappearance.

[Footage of police canvassing Hanwell neighbourhood]

They are also meticulously reviewing all CCTV footage of the area where she went missing, hoping to uncover clues previously missed.

Photos of Lucy are being posted prominently across the borough, and I want to appeal to any public member – please, if you know anything at all, even just a tiny observation, contact the police hotline immediately. Your information could prove vital.

I'm now joined by our correspondent Jason Clarke, taking over for Michelle Gray, who is getting a well-deserved break after reporting tirelessly from Hanwell. What's the latest there, Jason?"

[Split screen with Tara in the studio and Jason Clarke on the scene]

Jason: "Thank you, Tara. The mood is eager and anxious here as police blanket the neighbourhood pursuing leads. Officers are visible going door to door, following up on tips and asking if anyone saw anything suspicious before Lucy's disappearance.

Forensics teams are also examining physical evidence from locations along her walking route. CCTV from local shops and transit stations continues to be scrutinised frame-by-frame, though no breakthroughs yet. "

Tara: "Hopefully, the renewed activity and attention will release new information. Please keep us updated, Jason, as police continue looking under every stone in Hanwell to find answers. The entire nation remains invested in Lucy's safe return. "

LONDON, 03:31

Tara: "I've just received the latest police bulletin updating the situation with unrest across England:

[Map graphics highlighting locations of curfews, riots, protests]

[Police clash footage]

[Damage from looting/vandalism]

[Cancellation notices for events]

- Curfews remain in place across London and other significant cities experiencing riots. The curfew in Ealing and surrounding boroughs runs until 8 AM tomorrow, well, today.
- Over 1,000 arrests have been made nationally in connection with rioting and looting. One hundred officers have been injured responding to clashes.

- Hotspots like Brixton, Tottenham, and Manchester continue seeing. Incidents of violence, vandalism, and fires breaking out, straining police resources.
- Transport disruptions are still occurring, with all tube stations near Ealing remaining closed until 9 AM. Still, due to the impossibility of staffing trains and stations, the police recommend staying home where possible. Many bus routes are on diversion.
- Peaceful protests are also occurring in Nottingham, Leeds and other cities, calling for justice, police accountability, and immigration reform. These are being monitored but allowed to continue."
-

[She stops reading the bulletin]

Tara: "Peaceful protest deserves a forum. But unfocused violence will not hijack our airwaves when a child's life hangs in the balance. We reaffirm our commitment to keeping Lucy, not rabble-rousers, at the heart of this broadcast."

[She resumes reading the bulletin]

- The economic costs from property damage are still being tallied but will likely exceed £250 million across affected regions.
- Football matches, concerts and other significant events are being cancelled or postponed due to security concerns related to potential unrest.

That summarises the status provided by police on the riots and curfews enacted in the wake of Lucy Carver's abduction. A tense but contained environment as darkness continues across England tonight. It's now 3:33."

LONDON, 03:45

Jason: "Lucy's home where Lucy's parents, David and Elizabeth Carver, are about to hold a press conference to plea for information to help locate their missing daughter. But first, they plan to publicly apologise to Nikola Petkov for the mistaken accusations against him. Let's take it live now. "

[Exterior shot of the Carvers' home]

[Live feed of the Carvers seated, looking distressed]

David: "We want to express our deepest regrets to Mr Petkov for the false suspicion unfairly cast upon him.

[Photo of Nikola Petkov shown]

This is an unimaginably painful time for us, but it does not excuse what he went through. We are deeply sorry. "

Elizabeth: "If anyone knows anything to help bring Lucy home, please come forward.

[Elizabeth crying while making plea]

The last night without her has been agonising beyond words. Our baby must be so scared out there without us. We beg you not to hesitate to get in touch with the police if you have any information at all. We will never stop looking for our princess. "

David: *[choking up]* "Lucy. . . be a strong sweetheart. Your family loves you so much. We miss your smile lighting up our lives. Stay brave, and keep remembering all our happy memories together. We will bring you home. "

Jason: "A heart-wrenching plea from Lucy's parents, understandably distraught after the first night since her disappearance. Police have set up a dedicated hotline and continue pursuing all leads. But for now, Lucy's whereabouts remain a mystery, leaving the nation hoping tonight brings answers. "

Jason: "Police forensics teams are now meticulously combing Lucy's bedroom and personal belongings, looking for any evidence or clues. They are also working urgently to access and analyse her phone and online activity, hoping to uncover any communication that could provide leads. "

LONDON, 03:50

Tara: "In other updates, the Prime Minister is visiting Ealing to survey the damage from last night's riots and offer encouragement to police officers.

[Footage of Prime Minister touring damaged areas]

He reiterated his commitment to providing all necessary resources to aid in the search for Lucy. The Prime Minister vowed to restore order and justice for this local community and Lucy's family. No visit to the Carvers is planned. "

LONDON/BIRMINGHAM, 04:02

Tara: "I've just received an urgent bulletin from a national press agency that a video has emerged, possibly showing Lucy being forced into a car on her walk home from school yesterday.

[Graphic describing the video evidence]

[Silhouette recreation of video footage]

The video was submitted by an anonymous source and is said to show a young girl matching Lucy's description being pulled into a dark-coloured sedan around the time she went missing.

Police are analysing the footage right now to try to identify the make and model of the vehicle. While unconfirmed, this could be a significant break in the case if it is legitimate footage of Lucy's abduction.

Officers are working urgently to track down the vehicle and its owner as a potentially significant new lead. We will keep you updated if the video analysis provides any solid confirmation or clues for investigators to pursue. "

Tara: "Jason, what do you make of this potential video emerging showing Lucy's abduction?"

Jason: "If legitimate, it could be a pivotal break in the case that has yielded frustratingly few solid leads so far.

[Jason Clarke analysing video development]

However, we must be cautious until the footage can be authenticated and analysed correctly. I know the police will be working urgently to vet its validity and see if it provides any identifiable details on the vehicle or suspect. Like the rest of the country, I'm anxiously awaiting whether this pans out and gives investigators the traction they need to locate Lucy finally. "

Tara: "Absolutely, a note of caution until we know more, but the hope this could unlock answers. On another note, our livestream's audience on YouTube has now exceeded 50 million viewers globally.

[Graphic showing live viewer count over 50 million]

This clearly shows the incredible worldwide interest and concern focused on Lucy's case. "

Tara: "Rajesh, do you have any updates on Nikola Petkov now that he's been cleared?"

Rajesh: "Yes, Petkov is about to make a public statement shortly to address everything that has transpired. "

Tara: "Please interject live when he begins speaking. The world awaits his account. "

BIRMINGHAM/LONDON, 04:15

Rajesh: "Apologies for interrupting, but Petkov is now speaking. "

[Live feed switches to Petkov making statement]

Petkov: "This has been an unbelievable shock. . . to be accused of something so evil.

[Close-up shots of Petkov looking emotional]

I hold no grudges except against the police, who failed to correct the vehicle report that started this nightmare. I am an honest worker and taxpayer in this country. But I was presumed guilty only because of my foreign origin.

Certain people assumed the worst of me solely based on xenophobia and racism. The unjust profiling must end.

[Cutaway shots showing Petkov's sincerity]

And as for the senseless rioting and destruction, I saw the videos – it was opportunists and criminals, not people who genuinely cared about the girl. They exploited this tragedy to sow chaos and division at a time when hope and unity were needed.

It makes me sick to think the mob may have killed me if the police hadn't intervened. I just want my everyday life back after this trauma. And I hope for the sake of the little girl taken that you find the real criminal quickly. "

[The feed moves back to the studio and Rajnesh]

Rajesh: "Incredibly emotional words from Petkov, who made clear this unjust ordeal has turned his life upside down solely due to his immigrant status. Back to you, Tara. "

Tara: "Thank you, Rajesh. Our hearts go out to Mr Petkov, and we hope he can recover from this experience. Now, back to the search for answers. "

Rajesh: "Tara, Nikola Petkov has agreed to take some questions!"

[Split screen showing Rajesh and Petkov]

Reporter 1: "Mr Petkov, can you describe how police treated you while you were in custody?"

[Camera focuses on a reporter asking a question]

Petkov: "I was interrogated aggressively and doubted at every turn. They had presumed I was guilty from the start. "

[Petkov answering forcefully]

Reporter 2: "Do you believe authorities would have acted differently if you weren't an immigrant?"

Petkov: "Absolutely – I was targeted based on my background; there is no question about that. "

Reporter 3: "What long-term effects has this ordeal had on you mentally and emotionally?"

Petkov: "I don't think I'll ever fully recover from the trauma of what was done to me. My life will forever carry this stain of false accusation. "

Reporter 4: "What message do you have for the immigrant community in the UK right now?"

Petkov: "We must not let hate and prejudice push us into the shadows. Stand tall in yourself, do good, and improve this country. "

Rajesh: "Certainly some hard-hitting questions for Mr Petkov after his harrowing ordeal. As an immigrant, I sympathise with how he was unfairly targeted and presumed guilty. "

Tara: "I found his answers incredibly thoughtful, given what he experienced. He seems to hold slight bitterness, only a desire for justice and unity. "

Rajesh: "One wonders if authorities would have acted more cautiously if he wasn't an immigrant. A concerning double standard, perhaps. "

Tara: "I wish we could ask police leadership if racial profiling skewed their judgment and urgency in Petkov's pursuit. "

[Shot of Tara looking concerned in the studio]

Rajesh: "That's an important question we should press them on when given the opportunity. Could implicit bias have led them down the wrong path?"

Tara: "Taking a break now. I'll leave you with some ads and back in 2 minutes. "

[Brief transition to commercial break graphic]

LONDON, 04:32

Tara: "We have a significant update in the investigation into Lucy Carver's disappearance. The video showing a girl believed to be Lucy pulled into a dark sedan is now being treated as authentic by police.

[Silhouette recreation of critical moment from video]

Advanced analysis of the footage identified the make and model of the vehicle as a 2009 Ford Mondeo. More importantly, while grainy, the video reveals a partial license plate number that investigators are urgently working to track down.

[Enhanced still image from video showing partial plate]

Police Commissioner Martinez held a brief press conference earlier to validate the video's credibility based on the forensic authentication processes conducted by specialists overnight. She indicated it represents the most promising lead in determining what transpired during the approximate 10-minute window Lucy went missing.

While not confirmed with absolute certainty, investigators operate on the premise that this footage depicts the abduction. And the race is on to trace the vehicle registration while clues remain fresh. A model and partial tag now available represents a pivotal advancement in the search, provided police can fully capitalise on the lead before the perpetrator covers their tracks further.

Beyond the video analysis itself, we also receive word from Jason Clarke in Hanwell that a friend of Lucy's has come forward at 9:30 PM with intriguing new information that may prove relevant to the investigation. "

Jason: "Thanks Tara. I've spoken directly with the father of 13-year-old Melanie Abrams, who was part of the drama club with Lucy and came forward yesterday with information that could have aided the investigation much sooner.

John, Melanie's dad, claims that his daughter told police as early as 9:30 PM that Lucy confided in having an older secret boyfriend named Derek. However, investigators were so focused on pursuing the Petkov lead that they failed to promptly follow up on or circulate this revelation about this mysterious Derek figure.

Only after the direction on Petkov proved fruitless did authorities finally revisit Melanie's account given the previous night but not urgently pursued. Visited by the police at home in the aftermath of Petkov's blunter, she provided details about Lucy secretly meeting this older teen boy who may have been involved in her disappearance or have critical information.

Police are now actively investigating Derek's lead, but precious hours were lost due to the initial inaction after Melanie's timely report. Hopefully, Derek can still be identified and questioned over his association with Lucy, but the delay in pursuing this angle may prove costly."

[Silhouette figures representing Lucy and Derek meeting secretly]

Jason:" Derek is described as a brooding outcast-type who lived alone with his father on the other side of town.

While undoubtedly intelligent for a 10-year-old, Melanie says Lucy portrayed Derek as harmless but someone who made her feel mature and unique. However, Melanie admits she never met Derek directly; she just saw him at a distance and doubts that Lucy's parents or teachers knew anything about him.

Police are jumping on this lead now to identify Derek, verify the relationship, and investigate whether he had anything to do with Lucy's disappearance. Melanie provided the limited additional details she knew, including a physical description and the part of town he was said to live in.

Officers are already canvassing that neighbourhood looking for someone matching the description – a 17-year-old male with black hair and a lip ring named Derek who supposedly lives alone with his father.

While described as a secret boyfriend, the reality is that at ten years old, Lucy could have easily been manipulated or groomed by an older teen or someone pretending to be one. Police will tread carefully but take the revelation seriously as a promising new angle. "

Tara: "A potentially significant but concerning development if Lucy interacted secretly with an older teen online. Too often, these cases involve a child being expertly groomed by a predator posing as a friend or peer.

We can hope the relationship was innocent, but police must prioritise looking into this Derek figure – real or contrived – and his potential connection to Lucy's fate.

[Photo of Lucy, then split screen with silhouette of "Derek"]

And another police failure, there...

Thank you for the updates. We will keep following developments closely. "

Jason: "I'll add Tara that the community is reacting anxiously to this news. Parents are second-guessing if their kids also have online relationships they don't know about. Teachers are being pressed if they have seen any signs from Lucy.

Some blame themselves for not protecting her better against online harms. Others criticise the police for not uncovering this lead sooner. Lots of complex emotions swirling, on top of renewed hopes that this mysterious boyfriend could shed light on the truth. "

[Crowd shots and reactions]

Tara: "Understandable reactions, given fears around online predators these days. Our kids spend so much of their lives in digital spaces where dangers can hide in plain sight. Adults often struggle to keep up. But for now, the priority is identifying Derek and determining if he represents a truthful lead or distraction. We applaud the friend Melanie for having the courage to come forward. Vital information too often goes unreported due to stigma or shame.

Hopefully, her actions will inspire others to share any minute details that could potentially help authorities piece together this puzzle. Coming forward takes bravery, but it can make all the difference.

[Feed back to the studio]

We will keep probing sources for any additional updates related to tracing the vehicle from the video or verifying the existence and role of this mysterious Derek figure. Critical progress is happening. Let's stay optimistic. Lucy could soon be located safe, so this living nightmare for her family might end."

LONDON, 05:02

Tara: "Police are actively pursuing the lead on this mysterious Derek with whom Lucy allegedly had a secret relationship. However, analysis of her phone has not revealed any evidence of communication between them.

Investigators are now exhaustively reviewing CCTV footage along Lucy's route home, hoping to spot someone matching the description provided by her friend Melanie.

[Footage of police canvassing is shown]

Melanie firmly maintains she has seen Derek in person and believes she could identify him. With her parents present, she collaborated with a police sketch artist to create a composite image of his appearance.

That identikit sketch has now been published across local and national media outlets. Upon seeing it, the man appears older than 17 to me. Melanie describes pale skin, shaggy black hair, a lip ring, and a skull tattoo on his neck.

[Identikit of "Derek" is shown]

While the trail on Derek remains ambiguous, police are proceeding with an abundance of caution given the sensitivity of investigating a relationship involving a child. Melanie's parents are cooperating closely while ensuring she feels safe and supported. It's incredible how quickly the sketches were created and released!

Authorities continue analysing the video showing Lucy's abduction frame-by-frame for additional clues on the vehicle or suspect. This meticulous investigative process seems to yield promising advancements after earlier frustrations.

As always, police urge anyone who recognises this man or has any information about Lucy's disappearance to come forward immediately.

We applaud Melanie's bravery in assisting the investigation despite uncertainty around the validity of this mysterious boyfriend.

Hopefully, between the identikit, vehicle description, and enhanced video, detectives can soon close in on whoever is responsible for ripping Lucy away from her family and community. We will follow every development closely in the hunt to bring her home. "

5 – HOPE AMIDST DESPERATION

LONDON, 05:30

Michelle: “I’m now taking over reporting duties from Tara Jones, who admirably led coverage for over ten hours as this crisis unfolded.

[Feed on the correspondent Michelle Gray]

It has been roughly 12 hours since 10-year-old Lucy Carver first went missing.

In the wake of her abduction, riots and unrest have left hundreds of millions in damage, 8,000 arrests, one civilian death, and 130 police officers injured. The army continues patrolling Ealing and other affected areas.

[Montage showing damage and chaos from unrest]

The opposition is demanding resignations, from the Home Office to the Police Commissioner, over perceived mishandling of the investigation and response. However, the Prime Minister maintains they are doing everything possible and will conduct a review once the situation is resolved.

Tensions around the mysterious Derek lead are still high. Right-wing voices believe he is a fabrication to conceal the potential immigrant roots of the real kidnapper.

[Split screen with arguing pundits]

Another night of curfew is expected to be in effect across western boroughs, with trains by-passing stations in the borough of Ealing. The public is voicing frustration over the disruptions."

[Footage of empty streets and train stations]

[Resident frustrated over transport shutdowns]

Resident: "It's a disgrace they've shut down the whole transport network. How are we supposed to get to work or go about our lives?"

Michelle: "That sentiment from many as the lockdown continues. I'm also told Lucy's parents, David and Elizabeth Carver, will leave their home to visit the police station, likely seeking any updates.

[Footage of Lucy's parents departing their home]

We wish them strength during this torturous wait for answers on their daughter. Stay with us as our coverage continues through a long day."

LONDON, 06:02

Jason: "I'm outside the Ealing police station, where sources tell me Lucy's parents, David and Elizabeth Carver, have just arrived and entered the building. While unconfirmed, they may have some information relevant to their daughter Lucy's disappearance investigation. We will stay on scene here and report any updates after their meeting. A tense wait as perhaps critical new evidence comes to light."

[Camera shows the exterior of the police station, two worried parents walking up steps and entering doors]

Michelle: "Thank you, Jason. We'll look to get your live report later after the Carvers have met with the police. In the meantime, I'm here in the studio with a panel of experts to analyse this case..."

[Transition to news studio, Michelle seated at the desk facing three experts displayed virtually on monitors behind her]

Michelle: "I'm here in the studio with a panel of experts to discuss the ongoing abduction case of 10-year-old Lucy Carver, now missing for over 12 hours. With me virtually, we have a criminal profiler, Henry Frost, a legal expert, Claire Watson, and a child psychologist, Dr Linda Scott. Thank you all for joining.

[Experts nod/wave in acknowledgement]

Henry, from a behavioural analysis standpoint, what can you infer about the perpetrator based on the case details so far?"

Henry: "The deliberate nature of this abduction, yet lack of ransom demand, suggests a calculating offender motivated by deeper psychological compulsions. The target selection of a vulnerable child implies a predatorial figure observing victims and planning methods. An experienced criminal, yet one ruled by twisted urges."

[Continue discussion with visuals of Michelle engaging with experts, facial close-ups]

Michelle: "Claire, legally speaking, what charges would likely apply once a suspect is apprehended?"

Claire: "Kidnapping and false imprisonment of a minor would be foremost. Other charges, depending on circumstances, such as internet harassment if grooming was involved. Sentences can reach life in prison depending on factors like harm to the victim."

Michelle: "Dr Scott, what are the psychological impacts of abduction on a child like Lucy?"

Dr Scott: "Immense trauma stems from the act and removal from safety and family. Confusion, fear, and despair at her situation being out of her control. Possible manipulation by the abductor could further distort her emotions and sense of self. Extensive counselling would undoubtedly be needed to process the experience."

Michelle: "You all raise very incisive points. Expanding further, Henry, what does the abductor's selection of Lucy reveal about his motives?"

Henry: "Targeting a child shows a desire for power and control absent in healthy relationships. Victimizing the vulnerable feeds a complex inner sociopathy. This offender derives satisfaction from domination, inducing terror, and shattering innocence. A profoundly disturbed psyche is vainly seeking significance."

Michelle: "Claire, could you speak more about sentencing outcomes in cases like this?"

Claire: "Sentencing considers factors like harm to the victim, use of force or violence, planning, and other charges. Given Lucy's young age, length of confinement, and the suspect's likely history, a conviction could feasibly result in life in prison without parole."

Michelle: "Dr Scott, can you expand on the trauma Lucy may now be experiencing?"

Dr Scott: "Being removed from family support causes immense distress. Lucy is likely disoriented, experiencing constant anxiety about what her abductor might do. She may blame herself or struggle with the disruption to her normal childhood. Reconnecting to a sense of safety could take extensive therapeutic work on many levels."

Michelle: "How might identifying with her abductor potentially endanger her recovery?"

Dr Scott: "If she develops misplaced empathy or bonding with this criminal, it could profoundly skew her emotions post-recovery. She would need help recognising such distortions, restoring self-worth, and not accepting blame."

Michelle: "You all provide fantastic insights from your respective areas of expertise. To wrap up, what closing thoughts or advice would you offer regarding cases like Lucy's?"

Henry: "For law enforcement, a meticulous effort is key, but the perceptive analysis also helps unravel the suspect's motivations to aid in apprehension."

Claire: "The justice system must balance punishment, rehabilitation, and preventing future harm – an abduction conviction fully eliminates the chance for another."

Dr Scott: "For families and communities, unconditional support, compassion, and acceptance are critical to help these children regain trust and normalcy. Recovery takes time, but there is always hope."

Michelle: "Wise perspectives. Thank you again to our experts. Short break, then back with the latest on the search for Lucy Carver."

[Michelle is back online]

Michelle: "More expert insights into this tragic abduction case. Now let's return to Jason outside the police station for an update after Lucy's parents, David and Elizabeth Carver, met with detectives potentially sharing new information. Jason, what can you tell us?"

[Feed back to Jason in Hanwell]

Jason: "I'm still outside the Ealing police station where Lucy Carver's parents arrived earlier, potentially providing new information. While few details are available, in the last 15 minutes, we've observed an unusual flurry of police vehicles leaving the station, their sirens blaring as they speed off.

Most headed west toward Hanwell, where Lucy originally went missing. But others drove south towards South Ealing as well. It's unclear if these deployments relate to the Carvers' visit specifically.

However, the hurried urgency does suggest something pivotal may be unfolding today in the investigation. I conferred quickly with a few other journalists here. We collectively sense the elevated activity likely indicates fresh leads police are mobilising to pursue immediately. Precisely what those leads entail remains a mystery for now, of course.

But after the stagnation of recent hours, this feels like a long-awaited break that could hopefully take authorities closer to finding Lucy. There is a renewed energy amongst the press here, sensing we could be on the cusp of significant developments.

That being said, no crowds have gathered despite the flurry of activity. The cold night and ongoing curfew have kept most residents indoors, with Hanwell virtually deserted. Still, if concrete progress results from today's efforts, we expect a chorus of reactions once this community learns the details.

We can only read the tea leaves based on the hurried police deployments. But after so much fruitless searching, the urgency tonight implies potential evidence they can finally sink their teeth into. We will stay vigilant for any new information on where exactly these units have gone and why.

Hopefully, Lucy's parents provided the missing puzzle to reinvigorate this investigation. Or perhaps the police have unearthed a promising lead they are just now pursuing. Either way, we sense the winds may be shifting favourably today t in the hunt for answers."

Michelle: "Definitely positive signs if police actively deploy across Ealing on specific operations. While unconfirmed, it aligns with potential revelatory evidence from the Carvers' visit. We will keep monitoring your reports closely, Jason.

[Transition back to live exterior of police station]

In related news, I'm receiving word our producers got a call from a resident claiming he recognised the man in the sketch of the mysterious Derek figure linked to Lucy. He contacted the police as well to share more details.

It could be a monumental development if this witness has credible identifying information. Police forensic artists are highly skilled at rendering distinguishing features that spark recognition. We've seen it crack many cases before.

I want to clarify that we have not yet verified whether this man's claim is authentic. But our producers say he described concrete elements in the sketch – moles, ear shape, eyelid sag – that were not public knowledge. This lends early credence to his report.

Police will need to vet his account vigorously. But they may have a promising eyewitness on their hands. Combined with the intensified activity you're reporting, Jason, this case that seemed ice cold yesterday could be red hot tonight.

We will update you as soon as we learn more about this potential Derek identification. If legitimate, it hands police a name and face to pursue. That kind of solid intelligence, paired with the Carvers' information, represents the ingredients needed to solve a case.

I'm told detectives are actively following up on the identification lead now. Of course, they have pursued dead ends before, so restraint is warranted. But the palpable energy surrounding these latest developments injects renewed hope that Lucy could be located soon."

Jason: "I agree, Michelle. From my vantage point here this morning, it does feel like a major break in the case could be imminent. This community and country are desperate for it after the torment of recent days. The waiting game persists, but fingers crossed police make swift progress acting on these promising new leads. Our long national nightmare may be inching closer to resolution. We will keep watching closely."

[Camera pans over police vehicles racing out of station]

LONDON, 06:48

[Transition to news studio, Michelle at desk]

Michelle: "As we eagerly await updates on the new evidence police are pursuing this morning, let's recap some other top news headlines:

[Over shoulder graphic of temperature reading 6 degrees Celsius]

- Cold temperatures continue gripping most of England, with lows expected to plummet below freezing tonight and northerly winds adding an extra bite to the air.

Here in London, the mercury is around 6 degrees Celsius, prompting shelters to expand hours for people experiencing homelessness.

-

[Cutaway of person bundled up against cold walking down the street]

[Stock footage of British pounds and euros]

- In financial news, the pound sunk to a 6-month low against the dollar and euro amidst ongoing Brexit talks uncertainty. The Bank of England governor warned of a potential recession if a deal is not struck soon.

-

[Video clip of Bank of England governor speaking]

[Over shoulder graphic showing an uptick in COVID-23 cases]

- On the COVID-23 front, the Prime Minister announced expanded eligibility for vaccine booster shots as the UK reached over 150,000 confirmed cases. He urged the public to remain vigilant and raised concerns about the oncoming holiday season.

-

[Picture of PM gesturing during announcement]

- In entertainment, filming began this week on the sequel to the famous historical drama 'Victoria' detailing the life of the iconic Queen. It promises to cover her later rule and family tensions.

-

[Entertainment headline accompanied by photos from Queen Victoria show]

Those are just a few top national headlines, as the entire country remains transfixed on updates in the hunt for missing Lucy Carver.

[Transition back to Michelle at desk]

We will have the latest for you immediately once any new details emerge. Stay with us."

LONDON/SOUTHAMPTON, 07:13

Michelle: "We're interrupting this broadcast with breaking news. Our correspondent, Julia Scott, live in Hampshire, where an immigrant barge has been set ablaze by an angry mob protesting Lucy Carver's abduction. Julia, what can you tell us?"

[Transition to exterior dusk time view of Julia reporting near docks]

Julia: "Thanks, Michelle. I'm near the docks in Southampton, where a horrific scene has unfolded this morning. The 'Oslo Paradis' barge hosted over 500 asylum seekers looking to reach the UK, many fleeing conflicts in the Middle East and Africa.

[Over Julia's shoulder, show raging fire on barge, dark smoke billowing, people jumping off]

Around 6:50 AM, a group of approximately 30 wielding Molotov cocktails and flares approached the docked barge while shouting anti-immigrant slogans. Before authorities could intervene, they hurled their incendiary devices onto the deck, instantly setting it ablaze.

[Cutaway shots of angry mob, Molotov cocktails being thrown, courtesy of the public]

The group appeared organised, wearing masks and dark clothing. They carried signs condemning immigrants and accusing them of links to Lucy's disappearance. Based on this, police believe they planned this attack in retaliation for her case.

[Quick clips of anti-immigrant signs and chants]

Panic ensued on the barge as men, women and children were trapped by the intense flames ripping across the wooden vessel within minutes. The assailants cheered at the roaring fire and blocked its sole exit point.

Emergency responders raced to the scene but were overwhelmed by the sheer number of victims. Some passengers bravely jumped into the water to escape being burned alive. At least 50 serious injuries have been reported, but luckily, no confirmed deaths yet.

[Wide angle of multiple emergency vehicles, injured victims being treated]

With numerous fire crews battling the inferno, coast guard and harbour police boats began plucking victims from the water amidst the chaos and debris. The assailants attempted to flee, but most have been apprehended.

[Coast Guard boats rescuing people from water]

This area is in total lockdown now, with ambulances lined up to treat the wounded, several with critical burns. The air is thick with smoke billowing from the ruined, still-smouldering barge just a few hundred meters from me.

Authorities expect the number of casualties to rise as the situation stabilises tragically. The motive appears linked to anti-immigrant backlash over Lucy's abduction based on the incendiary signs and chants.

A heinous crime against innocent men, women and children fuelled by unproven suspicions over Lucy's case. We will continue providing live updates as rescue efforts continue through this devastating day."

Michelle: "Absolutely horrifying brutality carried out against these asylum seekers already fleeing trauma and terror. Julia, have police confirmed the attackers' identity or affiliations?"

[Return to Julia with smouldering barge behind her]

Julia: "Police have yet to release details, only confirming they have detained dozens of suspects. However, unofficially, sources tell me they have ties to far-right nationalist groups that have been fomenting much of the anti-immigrant backlash surrounding Lucy's case."

Michelle: "Any indication yet what prompted them to target this particular vessel at this specific time?"

Julia: "It seems this was a pre-planned retaliation in response to authorities pursuing foreign suspect leads in Lucy's case, contradicting the widely circulated sketch of the English boyfriend 'Derek'. These extremists took matters into their own hands to indiscriminately punish innocent immigrants."

[Transition back to Michelle in the studio]

Michelle: "And Julia, have you gotten any information from officials on whether this violence can be linked to broader underground networks?"

Julia: "That's still under investigation. But authorities suspect rogue elements of ultra-nationalist groups coordinated this attack, tapping into simmering xenophobia surrounding Lucy's case to incite more chaos."

[Over Michelle's shoulder, graphic with the headline "Immigrant Barge Attacked"]

Michelle: "Truly appalling. Please stay on top of this developing situation. Our hearts go out to the victims targeted by this unconscionable violence and hatred."

[Transition to the exterior night view of Julia for more details]

Julia: "I will provide further live updates as rescue efforts continue. It is a horrific scene but also shows courage and resilience in terror. Back to you, Michelle."

[Return to Michelle in the studio looking distressed]

Michelle: "Thank you, Julia. On top of Lucy's agonising case, this attack reflects dangerous divisions plaguing our country. More soon as we learn about potential casualties and those accountable."

LONDON, 07:43

[Transition back to studio, Michelle at desk]

Michelle: "We have the Home Secretary and the shadow home secretary with us to comment on the latest events. This was planned before we heard about the Oslo Paradis."

[Split screen with Home Secretary Hayes on the left, Shadow Home Secretary Roosevelt on the right]

Michelle: "Secretary Hayes, how do you respond to criticism that government immigration policies and rhetoric made minorities scapegoats, contributing to these extremist attacks?"

[Michelle facing monitors, engaging with each guest]

Home Secretary Hayes: "Our controlled immigration policies are balanced and necessary. We cannot excuse those who terrorise the vulnerable, whatever their stated grievances."

Shadow Home Secretary Roosevelt: "But your hostile stance fuels the view of immigrants as 'invaders' who provoke xenophobia. Reforms supporting assimilation over discrimination are vital."

[Tight shot of Michelle asking question]

Michelle: "And Secretary Roosevelt, what additional oversight around radicalization online would you support?"

Shadow Home Secretary Roosevelt: "We need greater monitoring of hate groups across platforms and fines for algorithms driving extremist content. Free speech protections cannot enable violence."

Home Secretary Hayes: "Censorship is a slippery slope, but we agree Big Tech must be held accountable for hate it profits from."

Michelle: "Turning to policing, harsh crackdowns on immigrant communities in response could further inflame tensions. How do we ensure a balanced response?"

Home Secretary Hayes: "Police must focus on individuals

instigating violence while building trust through greater community engagement."

[Wider angle showing all three in split screen]

Shadow Home Secretary Roosevelt: "Such incidents also spotlight their failures to disrupt these organizations before attacks occur. We need an independent review of far-right surveillance."

Michelle: "Finally, what lessons emerge from the unjust pursuit of the Bulgarian man and subsequent unrest it triggered?"

Shadow Home Secretary Roosevelt: "It confirms that institutional biases and unrestrained profiling based on migrant status breeds injustice and strife."

Home Secretary Hayes: "While mistakes were made, we cannot excuse the public taking the law into their own hands. Calm discourse, not destruction, must prevail."

Michelle: "Home Secretary Hayes, regarding Lucy Carver's case, police seem to be pursuing promising new leads this morning related to evidence from her parents and a potential suspect identification. Do you have any insight from briefings on where the investigation stands?"

Home Secretary Hayes: "I cannot comment on an ongoing investigation, but I'm encouraged by reports of renewed activity and progress after previous setbacks. We must allow detectives to follow this diligent process."

Shadow Home Secretary Roosevelt: "The public deserves transparency after the blunders compromising trust so far!"

Michelle: "And specifically on the horrific barge attack in Southampton, how do you interpret the motives and aim of this nationalist group?"

[Graphic over Michelle's shoulder with photos from barge attack]

Home Secretary Hayes: "A clear effort to terrorise and punish immigrants by exploiting anger over Lucy's case. Such hatred affronts British values and the rule of law."

Shadow Home Secretary Roosevelt: "Yet your hostile migrant rhetoric helps normalise such radicalisation and dehumanisation!"

Michelle: "How can security services detect and pre-empt such attacks before they occur?"

Home Secretary Hayes: "By enhancing coordination between law enforcement and intelligence agencies to identify threats earlier and share information proactively."

Shadow Home Secretary Roosevelt: "But they failed miserably to disrupt these actors previously, despite overt warning signs!"

Michelle: "Final thoughts on overcoming divisions so national harmony can be restored?"

Home Secretary Hayes: "Through compassion for all people, celebrating diversity, and marginalising – not amplifying – extremist voices who thrive only on hatred."

6 – UNFOLDING EVENTS

LONDON, 08:15

Michelle: "I have some new critical information about the suspect police identified as potentially behind Lucy Carver's disappearance.

[Photo of initial police sketch]

Earlier reports indicating Lucy had secret online contact with the man were incorrect. Lucy had no social media presence whatsoever.

[Graphic clarifying this revelation]

The suspect was recognised by Lucy's father, David Carver, as the father of a former patient who tragically took his own life last year. That man blamed Dr Carver for his son's death.

Upon showing the police sketch to David Carver, he immediately identified the man as this aggrieved father seeking retribution against him and his family.

[Footage of David Carver reacting to the sketch]

Reviewing surveillance footage supports this – the man is seen walking ahead of or in front of Lucy multiple times. They appear to interact and stop to talk briefly, where cameras don't cover.

[Surveillance footage showing interactions]

This has led investigators to reconsider whether Lucy was abducted unwillingly. They now suspect she may have voluntarily accompanied the man without understanding his true vengeful motivations.

[Police re-evaluating evidence]

The police-organised search continues for this suspect, now believed to be Lucy's father's former patient's dad holding a grudge. However, the latest evidence indicates Lucy could have left with him willingly before realising any danger.

This raises the hope that Lucy could be found alive and unharmed if located soon, though time is critical. I'm told the Carver family is shocked and devastated that their daughter may have been targeted in retaliation against them."

Michelle: "We're interrupting this broadcast to bring you breaking news out of Dover, where police have just descended on the port after a possible sighting of the key suspect in Lucy Carver's disappearance and a young girl.

[Live footage from Dover showing police swarming the port]

Our correspondent, Jean Charles, is live at the scene. Jean, what can you tell us?"

Jean: "Thanks Michelle. There is a massive police presence here at the Port of Dover after a man and young girl matching the suspect's description and Lucy Carver were spotted boarding a ferry headed to Calais, France, just over an hour ago.

[Overlay map of ferry route from Dover to Calais]

The call came to police around 7:25 AM from a concerned truck driver who recognised them from the nationally circulated suspect sketch.

[Photo of police sketch next to footage of truck driver calling police]

He reported seeing the man purchasing ferry tickets with cash while an unassuming red-haired girl who looked to be about ten years old stood nearby.

According to the trucker, they avoided eye contact and did not rouse suspicion from ticket agents or guards before being allowed to board with other passengers. The ferry departed at 8:05 AM with 300 passengers, and the girl was not heard from during boarding. Even here, it is unclear why the police didn't block the ferry from sailing.

When police flooded the port and sealed the area, the ferry was already out to sea. Authorities then scrambled all available naval assets while contacting French border control to be on alert for the vessel's arrival in Calais in just over an hour from now.

The captain has been made aware of the situation as police helicopters maintain visual contact trailing the ship as it crosses the Channel. To avoid alerting the suspect, authorities have temporarily deactivated data services, mobile signals, and the on-board TV broadcast on the ferry. Our live online broadcast has also been temporarily suspended for this sensitive operation portion. So far, there is no indication that the suspect is aware his presence has been detected as the ferry continues through the night in a communications blackout.

From what police tell me, their leading theory is that this man, identified as potentially connected to Lucy's case, was attempting to smuggle her out of the country covertly by water to evade the extensive law enforcement bulletins at airports and train stations.

Dover, a sprawling, busy port with thousands of daily travellers, allowed them to slip through unnoticed with fake or stolen identities. However, that plan seems to have been thwarted now, thanks to the sharp-eyed trucker.

Of course, police still cannot confirm with 100% certainty that the girl spotted is Lucy. However, all indications indicate a high probability based on her appearance and age. The fact she was compliant and not distressed has raised hopes she may be unharmed, though time is now of the essence.

With the vessel rapidly approaching French waters, authorities are coordinating an emergency operation with their cross-Channel counterparts to intercept it upon arrival in Calais approximately 50 minutes from now.

Coast guard and police boats are speeding to rendezvous with the ferry and board it forcefully, if needed, as soon as it drops anchor.

[Marine units shown speeding toward ferry route]

Meanwhile, a ring of security will surround the port to prevent the suspect from escaping into France with Lucy.

Police have requested we avoid showing live footage of their marine units so as not to inadvertently warn the suspect through our broadcast, even if, I repeat, there is no cellular signal on the ship, and no TV is available to passengers. However, I can describe a massive show of force now converging around the ferry's destination.

This includes at least six police cutter vessels alongside a pair of rigid inflatable boats with special operations officers onboard.

[Footage of police boats and armed officers]

Two French police helicopters are also inbounded to provide aerial support and surveillance.

[Police helicopters hovering over Channel]

They hope to quickly isolate and apprehend the suspect without resistance or jeopardizing other passengers' safety. But armed commandos are prepared for any outcome when they storm the ferry and scour it deck-by-deck at sea.

I'm told similar interdiction tactics were used in a hostage rescue mission five years ago in the Mediterranean. However, taking down a suspect quietly amidst 300 innocents onboard presents immense challenges, even for elite police units.

In the best-case scenario, they identify and extract the suspect within minutes before he can react violently or make demands. But this remains a hazardous time, an open-water operation that could quickly go awry.

While emotions are running high with Lucy potentially so close to being secured, authorities understand one misstep could turn this delicate mission catastrophic. However, they have no choice but to act swiftly with her life in balance.

So, in summary, races against the clock are unfolding on both sides of the Channel to safely retrieve Lucy from the grasp of this wanted man before they disappear into France. We will keep you updated constantly as this breaking situation develops..."

Michelle: "Incredibly fast-moving developments. Jean, is there any more information yet on how this suspect could board so easily with Lucy in tow?"

Jean: "Police are still piecing that together, Michelle. But they believe he presented forged identity documents for himself and Lucy that either appeared genuine enough or were inadequately verified amidst boarding chaos. Essentially, they slipped through the cracks thanks to lax oversight, which is inexcusable. However, authorities are already implementing emergency protocols to elevate traveller screening in response to this breach substantially."

[Footage of increased security checks at port]

Michelle: "And Jean, has there been any attempt to contact the suspect by radio or phone to negotiate Lucy's peaceful release?"

Jean: "Not as far as I know. Police seem to feel that could unduly provoke him without enough information on his mental state or intentions.

[Police conferring on tactical response]

Their priority has been covertly shadowing the vessel to be in position for a swift surgical intervention."

Michelle: "What has the public reaction been like since this news broke of a potential sighting?"

Jean: "Understandably, it's triggered a massive outpouring of anticipation and anxiety nationwide.

[Crowds anxiously awaiting news]

This apparent breakthrough has given hope that Lucy's ordeal could end.

Yet many also voiced anger that border officials failed to recognise and intercept them earlier. So, a mix of optimism and outrage as people process these rapidly unfolding events."

Michelle: "Jean, has there been any indication of this man's purpose in attempting to reach France with Lucy?"

Jean: "No clear motive established yet. But police suspect he may have wanted to extract her from the country where the search intensified to buy time plotting his next steps.

It's believed he acted impulsively after realizing authorities were closing in. However, his ultimate intentions regarding Lucy remain a mystery for now."

[Map showing suspect's movements]

Michelle: "Are there concerns he could have planted explosives or weapons onboard to use in the event of being cornered?"

Jean: "That's been considered; however, authorities say he passed through a security checkpoint and luggage screening like other passengers with no prohibited items found. It appears he prioritised avoiding detection over preparing an armed standoff."

Michelle: "And if this is the suspect and Lucy, how will you definitively confirm their identities to viewers?"

Jean: "I'm in direct contact with the police command overseeing the operation. They will relay a secure update to me as soon as identities are verified beyond doubt.

[Jean listening to police radio]

We will share that confirmation live once received from an

authoritative source."

Michelle: "One final question, Jean – what is the latest timing for when authorities expect to intercept the ferry?"

[Counter ticking down to projected ferry arrival time]

Jean: "The projected arrival remains 10:10 AM local time, that is 9:10 UK time. So, just under 30 minutes from now. Coast guard cutters should establish visual contact within 20 minutes of arrival, allowing encircling time. So, we are less than an hour from resolution theoretically."

Michelle: "Thank you for vividly portraying this dramatic law enforcement mobilisation. Please stay safe at the port but keep us constantly updated on any developments as they race to apprehend this suspect and ensure Lucy's wellbeing."

Jean: "You've got it, Michelle. I'll provide live updates as soon as we have them. A delicate, urgent situation is unfolding, and we hope to have positive news to share soon that Lucy is finally safe and sound after her long ordeal."

Michelle: "Viewers, as we closely monitor the maritime interception operation playing out in real-time, keep in mind many vital questions remain unanswered...

[Split screen showing Michelle in studio and police boats at sea]

Why did this person abduct Lucy? Is he rational and likely to comply peacefully? How has Lucy's health – mental and physical – been impacted?

We can only speculate until officials establish direct contact and bring them into custody safely. While we all pray for an uplifting outcome, this remains a highly unpredictable scenario.

We'll return to Jean shortly in Dover once the ferry nears Calais. But first, let's get perspective from our panel of experts standing by to analyse these fast-moving developments."

[Introducing expert panellists]

Michelle: "Joining me now for analysis of today's developments are criminal psychologist Dr Thomas Vega, legal expert Claire Watson, and former FBI hostage negotiator Daniel Lopez. Thank you all for weighing in.

[Headshots of each guest expert]

Dr Vega – From a psychological standpoint, how do you expect the suspect to respond when confronted by police?"

Dr Vega: "Given the unpredictability of his behaviour so far, he may react irrationally and aggressively if cornered, posing a substantial risk to Lucy and authorities."

Michelle: "Claire – Legally, what charges could he face?"

Claire: "With a minor victim, charges would include kidnapping, child endangerment, custodial interference, and potentially others depending on the circumstances."

Michelle: "Daniel – Based on your experience, how should police engage to ensure a safe resolution?"

Daniel: "The top priority will be guaranteeing Lucy's safety, likely through stealth and speed over negotiations. But compliance should be urged through de-escalation tactics first."

Michelle: "If force becomes necessary, what precautions can be taken to protect innocents nearby?"

Daniel: "They will isolate the immediate area around the suspect but avoid action that could spark wider panic. This requires incredibly tactical precision."

Dr Vega: "I would add that police need contingency plans accounting for every possibility given how unstable this offender appears. All bases must be covered."

Michelle: "Invaluable perspectives as we hope for a peaceful end to this crisis. We'll return to Jean in Dover for the latest developments when we return."

[Commercials broadcast]

Jean: "Welcome back. I'm here at Dover Harbour, but I have a colleague, Eric Du Fort, from Radio Calais, a local radio in the city where that ferry carrying the wanted kidnapping suspect and potentially Lucy Carver is now just 15 minutes from port.

The flotilla of police boats has the area surrounded with weapons trained on the channel exit. Snipers are positioned atop command vessels while helicopters circle overhead, waiting to swoop in.

The air is filled with tension, uncertainty, and hope. The French authorities are ready to act instantly once the target reaches range. This could be when Lucy is finally rescued if everything goes according to plan.

Eric is watching the horizon intently for any sight of the ferry. Thermal cameras can reportedly detect its engine heat signature.

[Camera footage tracking ferry]

Wait – I'm just receiving word from my source that French police have contacted the captain to prepare for immediate boarding upon docking. His response indicates the suspect still has no clue authorities are onto him.

Michelle, this advantage gives police a considerable edge for hopefully securing Lucy stealthily before violence erupts. Their element of total surprise may prove decisive.

Eric's vantage point prevents witnessing the takedown firsthand. But he can confirm the ferry lights are now visible to the naked eye, despite the fog on the Channel this morning. Just a few more agonising minutes until it comes into law enforcement custody.

He can discern flashing lights reflecting off the low clouds from multiple pursuers enveloping the vessel's rear.

[Flashing police lights on water ahead of ferry]

Their precise choreography reflects months of joint training for precisely this scenario.

The deafening silence is broken only by circling helicopters overhead. All eyes are glued to that speck of light growing more prominent on the grey waters. An entire nation, actually two, awaits the outcome along with Lucy's family.

We should be receiving confirmation any minute of the suspect's apprehension and Lucy's condition. This is the decisive moment we've waited on tenterhooks for as the ferry glides unwittingly toward capture.

[Suspenseful shot focused on approaching ferry]

Please stand by for live updates as soon as I know the operation has commenced. Praying this nightmare is nearly over."

Michelle:" Thanks, both. Or should I say Merci, Eric? "

LONDON/CALAIS 09:31/10:31

Michelle: "I'm now joined by Léa Durand, an English-speaking journalist with Radio France International who is live at the Port of Calais awaiting that ferry's arrival.

[Split screen with Léa Durand in Calais]

Léa, describe the scene there as French authorities prepare to intercept the vessel."

Léa: "Thank you, Michelle. There is a massive police presence here, with at least 20 patrol boats encircling the harbour exit while snipers stand ready on the docks.

[Police boats surrounding ferry path]

[Snipers positioned at port]

Two helicopters circle overhead, their spotlights aimed at the horizon. The ferry is now just minutes away, with coastal radar tracking it approaching the boundary of French waters. As soon as it crosses that border, police will initiate the boarding operation immediately."

Michelle: "Have passengers been made aware of the situation unfolding?"

Léa: "No, authorities have only discreetly notified the captain to avoid panic. Teams in full tactical gear wait to sweep the decks in a swift, surgical manoeuvre focusing only on the suspect."

Michelle: "What contingencies are in place if the suspect refuses to surrender?"

Léa: "Sharpshooters have authorization for lethal force only if lives are at risk. Otherwise, negotiators will urge a peaceful resolution. But they are prepared for any outcome."

Michelle: "And Léa, how will they secure young Lucy amid this confrontation?"

Léa: "That procedure is highly sensitive, given her trust in the suspect. Specialists will approach in plainclothes, identify themselves quietly, and escort her to safety before action against the kidnapper."

Michelle: "One final question – have French officials speculated on why Calais was chosen as the destination?"

Léa: "They suspect the dense refugee population here would have made disappearing easier. But police have flooded the port area to prevent any escape."

Michelle: "Thank you for the vivid account. Please update us on any developments as this historic cross-border operation enters its final phase."

[Commercial breaks]

Michelle: "I believe Léa Durand is ready with an update on the ferry interception operation. Léa, what's happening now as authorities prepare to board?"

Léa: "The ferry is now being approached by police boats with lights flashing. Officers are taking tactical positions on the exterior decks as the ship slows to a halt.

The captain is feigning normal operations so as not to alert the suspect. The order has been issued for police to storm simultaneously on all levels and converge on the suspect's location provided by the captain.

[Police stealthily boarding ferry exterior]

Sharpshooters have their rifles trained on the lounge windows where we believe the kidnapping suspect and Lucy are holed up. A pair of negotiators in civilian dress wait, ready to appeal to Lucy once the suspect is apprehended."

Michelle: "Have authorities formulated a plan to extract Lucy, given her trust in the kidnapper safely?"

Léa: "Yes, the priority is neutralising the suspect swiftly before addressing Lucy calmly, non-threateningly. The negotiators will reassure her that they intend only to reunite her with her family."

Michelle: "Will police use force if the suspect refuses to stand down?"

Léa: "Lethal force has been authorised if lives are directly at risk and no other option. But they will pursue de-escalation for a peaceful surrender if possible."

Michelle: "And what extra precautions are being taken to shield other passengers once the operation commences?"

Léa: "The captain has discreetly asked passengers to remain in their cars or stay in the main hall for their safety. Officers will focus solely on the kidnapper to avoid wider chaos or panic on board. But this will be hard to manage and justify to unaware travellers."

Michelle: "It seems we are nearing the pivotal moment as teams get into position. Please update us the instant police storm the cabin and try to secure Lucy."

Léa: "You'll have live coverage as this dramatic confrontation unfolds. An eerie calm before the storm now as hearts pound on both sides of the Channel. We stand ready."

[Another commercial break]

Léa: "This is Léa Durand reporting live from Calais. French police units have just forcibly boarded the ferry and appear to be initiating the raid on the suspect's lounge area.

[Live footage of raid commencing]

Armed officers are swiftly converging on the lower deck location identified by the captain. Two snipers on the upper deck have their rifles trained on the door, prepared to provide covering fire.

Bullhorns shatter the silence, ordering the suspect to exit with his hands up or face an immediate breach, and only 30 seconds is allowed for compliance.

No movement yet from within the cabin. Police are counting the final 10 seconds until dynamic entry and apprehension..."

[Shouts heard over a bullhorn, followed by a loud bang]

Léa: "Officers have just accessed the lounge and thrown in flash grenades to disorient any occupants! Muffled yelling can be heard from within as police storm the area!"

[Two gunshots ring out]

Léa: "Those were live rounds! Unclear if officers or suspect were fired! The operation is obscured from this vantage point. I can confirm that intense shouting and commotion are coming from the lounge."

[Sustained gunfire heard]

Léa: "A barrage of gunshots echoing from the scene! This has turned into a violent armed confrontation inside the Suspect's lounge!"

[Gunfire stops, followed by eerie silence]

Léa: "The flurry of shots concluded abruptly. All quiet now, no more discernible activity. Whatever climactic scene played out inside is over, for better or worse.

A row of ambulances waits shoreside – but no one has yet emerged from the lounge. Officers may secure the area or administer first aid if casualties result from the intense shootout."

Michelle: "Léa, can you confirm whether shots came from the suspect or were police responsible for the shooting?"

Léa: "Impossible for me to discern, Michelle. For now, it remains unclear who discharged firearms during those tense moments. Priority is ensuring the scene is stabilised."

[Stretcher seen carried by officers]

Léa: "A stretcher just came into view surrounded by officers – unclear if it carries the suspect or a team member. The indications are that someone has been injured or deceased.

Another stretcher is now being hurried from the lounge as well. Potentially facing severe casualties on either side here."

Michelle: "And no sign of Lucy yet?"

Léa: "None yet – outer decks have been cleared to evacuate any wounded. No confirmation of Lucy's presence or condition. We await first visuals of her emerging."

CALAIS/LONDON, 10:51/9:51

Léa: "Finally, some movement; I can see a female officer escorting a young redheaded girl wrapped in a blanket up the stairs from the cabin. It's Lucy Carver, alive! Repeat, Lucy is safe!"

[Footage of Lucy emerging escorted by officer]

Michelle: "Thank heavens. Léa, does Lucy appear physically alright?"

Léa: "She is visibly crying but can walk steadily with assistance. No overt trauma or bleeding. Responding calmly to the officer's encouragement."

[Lucy crying but walking under her power]

Michelle: "What an immense relief! She seems unharmed. Are negotiators present to help ease the transition?"

Léa: "Affirmative. A trained counsellor has joined them, speaking softly to Lucy as they make their way topside. She appears comforted by the woman's presence."

Michelle: "We're temporarily pausing our live coverage as events stabilise on the ferry. Let's take this opportunity to go to Tara Jones, who helmed our broadcast for the first long hours of this crisis before passing the baton.

[Split screen with Tara Jones reacting emotionally]

Tara, I imagine you are overcome with relief?"

Tara: "Without a doubt, Michelle. While many questions remain, knowing Lucy is safe after so many agonising hours of mystery is an incredible weight lifted. My heart leapt seeing her emerge on camera.

[Tara wiping away tears]

I felt as if part of my own family had been recovered. An emotional moment for all of us."

Michelle: "Absolutely. You formed such a connection to Lucy and invested so much in her return. This must be deeply poignant."

Tara: "It's difficult to describe... I barely slept, so consumed with concern for her welfare. To finally see indications she will be alright is the breakthrough we desperately hoped for but feared may never come. Amidst the chaos of recent hours, this uplifting development feels nothing short of a miracle."

Michelle: "While we, of course, temper our joy, knowing challenges lie ahead for Lucy, in many ways, this marks the end of the darkest period – the paralysing unknown surrounding her fate."

Tara: "Precisely. The worst torment was imagining where she might be or what horrors she might be enduring. At least now, regardless of what's been inflicted, there is solace she'll receive the support needed to mend."

Michelle: "From an investigative standpoint, authorities will be pressured to account for missteps and misjudgement over the last 14 hours. But now, we celebrate Lucy's liberation."

Tara: "Absolutely. There are plenty of hard questions ahead, but let's reserve this moment for relief and gratitude she was delivered from harm against all odds. My thoughts are with her family, anticipating that cherished reunion. Out of this tragedy, that unbridled joy will uplift us all."

Michelle: "Well said. Your poise and compassion these last hours have been a beacon. This is your moment as much as Lucy's after walking this excruciating journey alongside us."

Tara: "You're too kind. I'm just thankful we could comfort viewers and Lucy's loved ones struggling to endure the darkness and uncertainty. Faith and fortitude can see us through even the most hopeless nights."

Michelle: "Your inspiring words and steadfast presence helped sustain us. Today, your vigil has been rewarded. We could not have made it through without you."

Tara: "I'm humbled to have contributed, but the real heroes are those who tirelessly searched for Lucy, risking all. And amazing young Lucy, of course, for surviving with such grace and courage."

Michelle: "On that note, let's check in with our panellists: Dr Linda Scott, child trauma specialist. Daniel Lopez, former FBI negotiator, and Legal analyst Claire Watson for added perspective now that Lucy is safe."

[Introducing expert panellists]

Dr Scott: "I hope that with patient, compassionate support, she can overcome this and thrive. I'm optimistic seeing her calm response to counsellors, a good initial sign."

Daniel: "The most dangerous point was the initial raid when the situation could have spiralled. Thankfully, police controlled the scene to shield Lucy despite the suspect's resistance."

Claire: "Legally, the priority now is building an airtight case against all responsible while prioritising Lucy's healing and privacy above all."

Michelle: "Insightful as always. We're grateful to have such expertise helping us navigate an impossible ordeal these last days."

Tara: "Absolutely. Your wise counsel has been invaluable. It's easy to feel hopeless when the forces against you seem overpowering. But we must never surrender to darkness or vengeance. Light still flickers even when we cannot see it."

Michelle: "Well said, Tara. Your moving words and compassion will stay with us. We could not have made it through this crisis without your leadership."

Tara: "You honour me too much. This was a team effort; truthfully, Lucy did all the heavy lifting. Her inner spark pushed her through the darkest abyss. I'm just overjoyed her radiant light can now start shining brightly again."

Michelle: "On that uplifting note, we'll take a short break as this historic day unfolds. When we return, we'll return to Léa in Calais for the latest following Lucy's rescue. Finally, some joy pierced the clouds after so much anguish. Stay with us."

[Brief transition graphic to commercial break]

Tara: "Thank you, Michelle. However, if this unfolds, we will get through it together. Faith over fear. And justice for our beloved Lucy."

CALAIS/LONDON, 11:02/10:02

Léa: "Lucy is now being tended to in a secure area away from the crime scene. Multiple ambulances have since sped away, carrying injured officers or the suspect to hospital.

[Footage of ambulances departing]

A forensics team has entered the lounge now the threat is neutralised, beginning collection of ballistics and other evidence to reconstruct what transpired."

Michelle: "And has the suspect's condition or fate been disclosed yet?"

Léa: "Police remain tight-lipped so far, only confirming casualties without specifics. The body language of officers who engaged him suggests he did not survive the confrontation."

[Sombre officers at the scene post-raid]

Michelle: "A violent ending, but the priority is Lucy's welfare after her unimaginable ordeal. Léa, does it appear authorities succeeded in shielding passengers from the violence?"

Léa: "Fortunately, the tactical teams rapidly isolated the lounge. No other passengers appear caught up in the events. The ship will return to routine operations shortly."

Michelle: "What can you tell us about Lucy's demeanour since being freed from captivity?"

Léa: "Understandably, in a state of shock and confusion. She alternately sobbed into her hands and gazed ahead stoically. Counsellors maintain a comforting watch nearby as she processes the trauma."

[Lucy being comforted after ordeal]

Michelle: "Our hearts break imagining what she's endured. Please keep us updated on any statements from investigators or next steps for Lucy now that her recovery can finally begin."

Léa: "You'll have the breaking details live from Calais. After so much turmoil, let's take a moment to celebrate Lucy's liberation from this unthinkable nightmare against all odds."

LONDON, 10:33

Michelle: "We're just receiving word that Prime Minister Chelmsford will be making a statement shortly regarding Lucy Carver's rescue.

[Other news is read]

LONDON, 10:43

Prime Minister Chelmsford: "I am overjoyed to hear that brave Lucy Carver is safe and cared for after her harrowing ordeal.

[Split screen of PM address and Lucy recovery]

I commend the outstanding efforts by police on both sides of the Channel and offer my profound thanks to French authorities for their indispensable role in bringing Lucy home.

While serious inquiries lie ahead, today we celebrate an innocent life, sparing her loving family the most profound imaginable anguish. May Lucy heal surrounded by fierce support and find brighter days ahead."

Michelle: "The PM is voicing the palpable sense of national relief and goodwill following Lucy's liberation from captivity against all odds."

Michelle: "We're also told Lucy's parents, David and Elizabeth Carver, are being transported via an RFA helicopter directly to Calais to reunite with their daughter after this agonising separation. I cannot imagine a more emotional or rewarding reunion after helplessly enduring every parent's worst nightmare for over 16 hours. Our hearts overflow picturing the joyful tears and embrace awaiting."

Michelle: "Let's check in now with our own Jason Clarke in Hanwell for the scene there as news breaks that their hometown girl has been freed at last."

Jason: "Thanks, Michelle. I'm in Hanwell by the Clock Tower, where residents have gathered spontaneously to celebrate Lucy's rescue.

[Crowds cheering and celebrating in Hanwell]

Church bells are tolling, some are singing hymns, and an impromptu candlelight vigil is taking shape to show support in plain light.

The community is overjoyed, many with tears in their eyes. Having braced for the worst, this long-awaited affirmation of life has released a collective wave of euphoria. Knowing their beloved Lucy is safe, Hanwell can breathe easily after so much angst."

Michelle: "Scenes of jubilation mirroring those across the UK as we revel in this hard-won victory for law enforcement, but most importantly for Lucy and the indelible courage she has demonstrated these past days."

LONDON, 11:01

Michelle: "We're just receiving statements from Buckingham Palace conveying the Royal Family's delight at today's outcome:

[Buckingham Palace exterior]

'Her Majesty, the Queen Consort, offers heartfelt thanks to the police and joy over Lucy Carver's rescue. We wish her a swift recovery surrounded by loving support.

[Photos of Queen Consort and King Charles III]

His Majesty King Charles III declares: 'This triumph of compassion and tireless service proves that light overcomes the darkest evils.'

Touching reflections from the Queen and the King underscoring the national relief as we begin healing from these traumatic events now that Lucy is safe."

Michelle: "In a tragic contrast to today's celebration, we're learning the death toll in the Southampton immigrant barge arson attack has risen to 12 victims, including five children, with 24 others seriously injured.

[Footage and headlines related to Southampton attack]

Police confirm 26 arrests so far as they work to hold accountable all those linked to this unconscionable tragedy."

Michelle: "On a positive note, we expect some return to normalcy in the coming days:

[Montage showing curfew ending, trains resuming, road reopening]

- Curfews enacted across London boroughs will all cease.
- Trains running through Ealing will resume stopping at local stations beginning immediately as restrictions are lifted.
- Road closures and cordons around Hanwell should be removed, allowing regular traffic flow to resume.

Small but meaningful steps back from crisis footing as the investigation transitions from emergency to after-action phase."

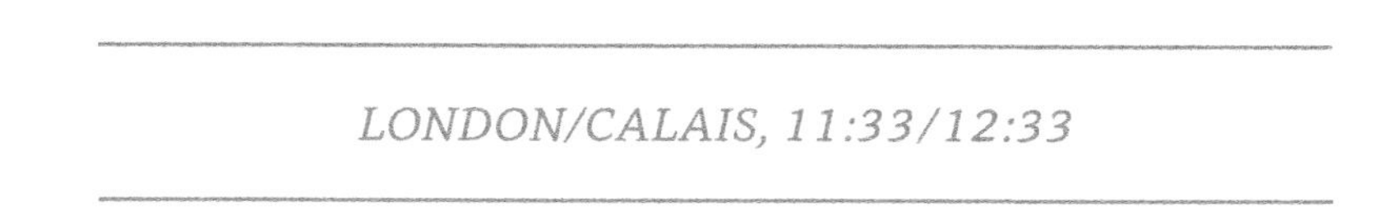

Michelle: "We're returning to Léa Durand in Calais for the latest developments following Lucy Carver's dramatic rescue earlier. Léa, has there been any official confirmation yet regarding the status or identity of the kidnapping suspect?"

Léa: "Authorities just held a brief press conference naming the deceased suspect as Hugh Langley, a 27-year-old Ealing resident believed to be the father of a former young patient of David Carver's who tragically took his own life last year."

Michelle: "That chilling motive fits with what investigators suspected. And Léa, how is young Lucy faring in the aftermath of her harrowing experience?"

Léa: "Physically, she shows no major injuries, thankfully. Emotionally, there is deep trauma evidenced by confusion, crying spells, and withdrawn body language. She has only briefly spoken about believing Langley was her friend."

Michelle: "Just heartbreaking. And what has been the reaction there in France to this dramatic cross-border case concluding on their soil?"

Léa: "Overall, a huge sense of relief, both at Lucy's safe return and the close cooperative efforts by police that led to this outcome. French officials are commending the coordination while pledging continued vigilance given the exploitation of Calais as an apparent destination."

Michelle: "A reassuring commitment to partnership from our allies across the Channel. Thank you for your stellar reporting, Léa, throughout this crisis."

Michelle: "That concludes our extended live coverage of the dramatic abduction and rescue of Lucy Carver. While this innocent child's recovery is just beginning, we can all sigh with relief knowing she is back in safe hands after her unimaginable ordeal.

[Photo of Lucy surrounded by support]

I want to sincerely thank our millions of viewers worldwide who tuned in anxiously awaiting updates and for all the messages of hope and compassion. Lucy's story touched so many.

Our outstanding correspondents and experts worked tirelessly to bring you the breaking details as this complex case unfolded across two countries over many harrowing hours. Their dedication was inspiring.

Of course, our most profound admiration goes out to Lucy herself. Her incredible bravery and perseverance in the face of grave terror deserve all accolades. She is truly a hero.

[Close-up of Lucy looking resilient]

Our regular news programming will resume moving forward now that young Lucy is free. I will sign off with immense gratitude in my heart.

Good day, and Godspeed to Lucy Carroll. Sorry, Carver. A little girl captive no more."

7 – EPILOGUE

["Vanished Echoes" appears on the screen behind the speaker with a depiction of Lucy, book in hand and London set ablaze behind her]

Jason: "Good evening, and welcome to London Prime News Network. It has been quite an eventful six months since our network's groundbreaking coverage of the Lucy Carver kidnapping story that gripped the nation.

While John Davis has retired, we have welcomed Chief Editor Tara Jones as our lead news anchor. Michelle Gray has moved over to anchor our expanded national nightly bulletin.

And I'm Jason Clarke, a newly appointed London anchor after reporting on the streets of London for over a decade. It's an honour to now lead our flagship broadcast.

Our full live coverage of Lucy Carver's abduction catalysed significant growth for Prime News. We have bureaus across England now while increasing our digital reach tenfold.

But most importantly, we hold the profound responsibility of providing urgent breaking news with compassion, accuracy, and insight. That legacy was cemented during the Lucy Carver saga.

Tonight, we present a new documentary by Tara Jones, looking back on that dramatic story through interviews and insights from critical voices. Tara, please introduce us to your film. "

Tara: "Thanks Jason. This documentary explores the issues and emotions during little Lucy Carver's nationally followed kidnapping last autumn.

We revisited the tense night and day of broadcasting live amidst the mystery and unrest. And the indescribable relief at Lucy's rescue against the odds, sparking reflection on mental health and social divides.

Most meaningfully, this is a tribute to a brave girl who endured profound terror yet persevered with inspiring grace. Lucy united millions in hope during her darkest hours. Her light shined on through the darkness. That is Lucy's everlasting triumph. "

[Images of the documentary are broadcast]

Tara: "Good evening, I'm Tara Jones from London Prime News Network, and before we get to tonight's weather forecast, we want to bring you some breaking news from the Hanwell area of Ealing in west London. "

[The voice fades]

Tara: "We are just receiving initial reports of a 10-year-old girl, identified as Lucy Carver, who has allegedly been abducted within the last couple of hours. Specific details are still minimal at this time, but here is what we know so far:"

"Lucy had been attending drama club at the Hanwell Community Centre after school today. According to her parents, she left around 5 PM to walk the short distance home, about half a mile away. "

[The voice fades]

Tara: "From what we know, police have begun interviewing Lucy's parents and friends from the drama club, looking for any clues on who she might have been seen with or anything suspicious noticed... "

[The voice fades]

Tara: “Lucy is described as 4’3” tall with long red hair. When she left the Community Centre, she was last seen wearing a black leather jacket, jeans, and a blue backpack.”

Tara: “Our news team dispatched correspondents to rush to the scene in Hanwell. We hope to have them there shortly to provide live updates. “

[The voice fades]

Tara: “Our thoughts are with Lucy’s family and the Hanwell community this evening. We can only imagine the anguish her parents must be experiencing right now with their daughter’s unknown whereabouts or condition. “

[The voice fades]

Tara: “The circumstances suggest we could be dealing with a child abduction here in our London area. “

[The voice fades]

Tara: “I’ve just received word our correspondent Michelle Gray has arrived at the Hanwell Community Centre. “

[The voice fades]

Tara: “That was the beginning of what turned out to be an extended live coverage on the day Lucy first went missing. As the situation unfolded over the following days, the nation became invested in her safe return.

Millions tuned in anxiously for updates as the mystery surrounding her fate deepened. And when she was finally rescued after so much agonising uncertainty, the collective relief was palpable.

For our broadcast team, it was a professionally and emotionally draining experience, but also our calling to serve the public good in a time of crisis.

We realised our unique position to provide comfort, hope, and truth.

As it turned out, young Lucy would go on to capture hearts worldwide with her incredible bravery and resilience through unimaginable terror. Hers is a story we'll never forget."

Tara: "The roots of this tragic saga begin with Benjamin Langley, the 8-year-old son of Lucy's kidnapper, Hugh Langley.

Benjamin took his own life at eight while struggling with severe childhood depression. Friends and family noticed drastic changes in his personality starting around age."

[Interview clip: Benjamin's teacher]

Teacher: "He went from being a bright, engaged student to withdrawing from activities and friends. We offered counselling support, but the light in him just faded. "

[Interview clip: Benjamin's friend Tommy]

Tommy: "We used to play football together every weekend. But he stopped showing up and would get angry if I asked to hang out. I didn't know what was wrong. "

Benjamin's mother Sylvia, who refused to be filmed, remembers her son's infectious laugh disappearing as he sank into despair despite her efforts to get him professional help. Their family felt powerless to ease his torment.

The inquest following his tragic suicide at only eight years old questioned Dr David Carver's psychiatric care of Benjamin leading up to his death. Dr Carver had prescribed medication but only saw Benjamin occasionally.

The coroner concluded Benjamin's severe childhood depression required intensive long-term treatment that he did not receive.

Our sources believe Hugh Langley fixated on blaming Dr Carver for this perceived failure to prevent his son's suicide at such a tender, vulnerable age.

Consumed by grief and misplaced rage over losing a young child, Hugh severed ties with the mental health services that tried to help Benjamin. He became a recluse focused on what he saw as avenging his lost little boy.

In Lucy Carver, he tragically found a young girl who became the undeserving target of Hugh's delusions of vengeance against her father, Dr Carver. "

Tara: "We now know Hugh was seeing Lucy in person without her parents' knowledge, taking care to avoid detection by surveillance cameras. "

[Show CCTV footage of Hugh and Lucy interacting briefly and then separating]

Tara: "As seen here, in an exclusive footage not available at the time, Hugh would intercept Lucy as she left activities and walk with her briefly while posing as a 17-year-old boy. Their meetings were kept hidden from Lucy's family. "

Criminal Psychologist: "This patient strategy of gaining incremental trust while evading witnesses or recordings speaks to an unnerving capacity for deception and cunning. "

Tara: "Hugh gave the impression of being a harmless teen mentor, deceiving Lucy into feeling safe in his company. But his sinister motivations lurked just below the surface, soon to rear their ugly head. "

Tara: "As the search for Lucy dragged on unsuccessfully, public frustration boiled over into widespread riots and unrest in Ealing and beyond. "

[Show clip of rioters looting shops]

Tara: "With tensions high, looters and vandals exploited the chaos across London, causing extensive property damage. "

[Show clip of clashes in Margate]

Tara: "In Margate, violent anti-immigrant protests erupted, with police struggling to maintain order. "

[Show aftermath of Ealing town hall explosion]

Tara: "Most tragically, a bomb exploded at the Ealing town hall, claiming the life of a Nigerian cleaner, Taope Ngene, and mother of three children. Sowing more division at a time of heightened emotions. "

David Carver: "My wife and I were sickened by the violence and destruction occurring when people should have united to find Lucy. An innocent woman died – all while Hugh still had our baby hidden away somewhere. "

Tara: "Amidst the escalating turmoil across the country, the search for Lucy pressed on. But answers remained elusive, allowing a dangerous criminal to continue evading justice. "

[Interview clip: right-wing protester]

Protester: "The immigrant invasion led to this girl getting snatched. But did authorities crack down on them? No, they locked us down with curfews and arrests while another migrant probably skipped town with the kid.

Tara: "Fringe voices used Lucy's case to amplify xenophobic rhetoric and advanced anti-immigrant agendas – never mind the facts. "

[Show footage of imposed curfew and cordoned-off Ealing]

Tara: "And as the search continued without progress, officials instituted unprecedented security measures like overnight curfews and isolating Ealing entirely from outside access."

David Carver: "Imagine our desperation and helplessness during the curfew with nowhere to search and no updates. We felt so powerless while our only child was in the hands of a monster. "

Tara: "The increasingly severe lockdown fuelled tensions while doing little to aid the investigation. But authorities claimed public safety necessitated it. "

Nikola Petkov: "I was heading to football when police surrounded me, guns drawn, ordering me out of my friend's van. They wouldn't listen to anything I said, immediately putting me in handcuffs."

[Show dramatic footage of Petkov's arrest]

Nikola Petkov: "They interrogated me for hours, accusing me of taking Lucy Carver. I kept pleading my innocence, but the more I denied it, the more aggressive they became."

[Show footage of Petkov after his release]

Nikola Petkov: “After the longest night of my life in jail, they finally confirmed I had nothing to do with this girl’s disappearance and let me go. They did not even apologise after the hell I went through because of their mistakes and failures. I was terrified but heartbroken that the real kidnapper was still free for Lucy and her family. “

Tara: “Just when hope faded, a shocking development occurred hundreds of miles from the search area that changed everything. Melanie, a brave teenage friend of Lucy, opened a new trail. The police neglected the initial report because they were sure Petkov was the culprit. ”

Tara: “I was astonished when the urgent call came in that Lucy and her abductor may have been spotted trying to secretly board a ferry to France in the port town of Dover. “

Jason: “The crucial tip came from a lorry driver named Malcolm Wells, who was queued at the Dover terminal that morning. He recognised the pair from the wanted posters before they disappeared onto the departing ferry amongst the crowd. “

[Interview clip: Malcolm Wells, tipster]

Malcolm Wells: “As soon as I spotted that red-haired girl with the sketch bloke, I knew I had to alert the police immediately. I wasn’t about to let her disappear. “

Léa Durand: “I’ll never forget the sight of elite police units storming that ferry to rescue Lucy finally. After so much turmoil, seeing hope prevail was an unforgettable moment.”

[Show footage of the raid by the French gendarmerie and special forces]

Léa: “The entire continent watched breathlessly as this cross-border operation unfolded, hoping young Lucy would emerge unharmed. Against all odds, she did. "

Tara: "We now know Hugh Langley obtained false passports for himself and Lucy months beforehand, enabling them to book ferry tickets under assumed identities without raising suspicion. "

Léa Durand: "The elaborate planning and illegal documents secured well

In advance, further demonstrate the premeditation behind this plot. Still, how they could get through controls so easily is unclear."

Tara: "In the aftermath, the national police commissioner resigned over failures that allowed Hugh to escape the country with Lucy. The Home Secretary also stepped down amidst a scandal over missed opportunities to apprehend Hugh earlier. "

Jason: "Tragically, complacency and lack of vigilance at multiple levels made this situation spiral out of control, ultimately putting Lucy's life at risk. There were profound institutional shortcomings. "

Tara: "We met Lucy at her family's home, where she spoke candidly about her recollection of events. "

[Interview clip: Lucy Carver]

Lucy: "I thought Hugh was my friend. He would visit after school and tell me secrets my parents would not understand. I know he was tricking me, but I believed everything he said. "

Tara: "Lucy described how her supposed 'friend' gradually gained her trust before convincing her to come with him. "

Lucy: "That day, he said we'd go on an adventure where no one could bother us. I shouldn't have gone, but he promised it would be fun and I'd be back quickly. I didn't want to upset him. "

Tara: "Once separated from the safety of family and community, the facade slipped away. "

Lucy: "Initially, he was still lovely, driving and buying me gifts. But after a while, he started getting upset quickly, yelling that my dad was to blame. I got scared being alone with him. "

Tara: "However, Lucy's resiliency persevered despite the evolving nightmare. "

Lucy: "I just kept praying my family would find me. Whenever he left the car, I searched for a way to escape. I knew I had to stay strong to get back home. "

Tara: "Lucy was unable to disclose full details of abuse suffered. But professionals say cases like hers often involve severe manipulation and trauma. "

Child Psychologist: "Perpetrators use psychological coercion and deceit to dominate their victims. This induces deep confusion, anxiety and damage to self-worth that can linger. "

Lucy: "We never stayed anywhere inside. Derek, Hugh said we were taking a long drive to Disneyland Paris as a surprise fun trip my parents would meet us at. I realise now he was lying, but I believed him then.

Tara: "Lucy says they remained in the car at motorway service stations overnight as Hugh continued deceiving her that they were en route to a magical vacation rather than an abduction. "

Lucy: "He let me pick snacks and gave me stuffed animals from the gas stations. I did not think anything was wrong. Well, I did, and then I did not. He just kept saying we were getting closer to Disneyland and the big surprise. "

Tara: "In reality, Hugh was biding time as the police search spread looking for them. "

Lucy: "I kept wondering when we'd get there and asking if we could call my parents. He'd get mad whenever I asked about it. That's when I started to get scared. "

Tara: "When the critical moment came, Lucy reacted with courage beyond her years. "

Lucy: "I heard shouting and loud bangs from where Hugh had told me to hide. I was terrified, but then the police rescued me. I didn't want to let go of the nice officer's hand."

Tara: "Lucy described the challenges she still endures following her recovery. "

Lucy: "I have nightmares he's coming back, and no one believes me. I talk to my counsellor about it a lot. She says I'll feel better once he can't ever hurt me again. "

Tara: "Police later informed Lucy of Hugh's demise. But the light still pierces the lingering darkness. "

[Lucy is shown playing joyfully]

Lucy: "I know my family will always keep me safe now. And so many people cared about what happened. I want to help other kids not feel afraid or alone like I did. "

Tara: "A living profile in profound courage – Lucy's story of resilience continues inspiring the world. "

Tara: "The world watched Lucy's rescue unfold in real-time. But only she knows the whole truth of what was endured during captivity at the hands of her tormentor. "

Tara: "I'll never forget seeing Lucy emerge frightened but alive. Yet we knew the real battle was beginning to help her heal emotionally. "

[Lucy is shown playing with dolls, then contemplative]

Lucy: "When I think back to my days with Hugh, it feels like a nightmare I can't wake up from. But talking about it helps make sense of things. "

Tara: "Behind closed doors, the arduous path of healing had only begun for Lucy upon her return home. "

[Lucy is shown happily playing with her parents]

David Carver: "The joy of having Lucy back in our arms was overwhelming. But it soon became clear there would be many challenges ahead. "

Elizabeth Carver: "She'd have intense night terrors and anxiety attacks triggered by memories. We took her to top specialists, but what helped most was our unconditional love. "

Tara: "The Carvers describe a winding road to recovery filled with progress and setbacks. "

David Carver: "Weeks could go by without incident; we'd think the worst was behind us. But trauma has a way of resurfacing when you least expect it. "

Elizabeth Carver: "No matter what, we never gave up hope. There were dark days, but Lucy knew she had her family beside her. With time, the light returned to her smile more consistently. "

Tara: "The Carvers chose to shield Lucy from the furore unfolding nationally in the aftermath. "

David Carver: "There was an angry public reckoning over perceived failures by police and politicians. We tuned it all out to focus only on Lucy's wellbeing. "

Elizabeth Carver: "Our neighbours were excellent, giving us privacy and supporting however they could. The community rallied around Lucy. "

Tara: "In the wake of missteps, authorities instituted significant reforms to prevent such breakdowns again. "

[News clips showing officials resigning, protests]

Tara: "Public figures fell. Policies changed. But for the Carvers,

Lucy's recovery took priority over everything. "

David Carver: "Nothing could fully erase our little girl's trauma. But kindness, therapy, and above all, love – those forces helped her greatly. We saw our real Lucy emerging again."

Tara: "Amidst the broader turmoil, their devotion never wavered. "

Elizabeth Carver: "There were still hard days sometimes. But we learned to take each one as it came. Every smile, every laugh, was a reminder of light triumphing over darkness."

Tara: "Producing this retrospective was a very emotional experience for our entire team. We relived the sleepless night covering Lucy's case, not knowing if she would be found alive. The jubilation when she was rescued against all odds. And the harrowing journey we witnessed as she found her way back to happiness.

This was not just a breaking news story for us – it was deeply personal. We bonded with the Carver family, celebrated Lucy's strength, and felt invested in her recovery. Over 15 straight hours live on-air, we experienced every twist and turn alongside the viewers, depending on our coverage.

This documentary allowed us to reflect on that whirlwind experience. We realised our broadcast gave a voice to the voiceless and hope when it was needed most. It revealed divisions in desperate need of healing. But above all, it amplified a brave young girl who stirred the soul of a nation."

[Show footage of news team at award ceremonies]

"Our nonstop coverage earned recognition from peers, validating our principles of truth, compassion and integrity in journalism. "

"But the most tremendous honour was helping give Lucy's story a platform to touch lives worldwide. "

[Show footage of Lucy laughing and playing]

"With darkness, she persevered, and with light, she triumphed. Her unrelenting spirit united millions. Even in uncertainty, her courage ignited belief. She emerged forever changed but unbroken.

That is Lucy's legacy – a guiding star reminding us that hope always shines bright if we dare to see it. "

8 – CLOSING THOUGHTS

[The author is sitting in front of a camera in an empty TV studio]

Luigi Pascal: "As we conclude this televised account, I wish to acknowledge that the preceding story and characters are entirely fictional.

Through this dramatised narrative, I intended to underline the societal issues that presently grip Britain – a nation of escalating division and eroding compassion.

In the climate reflected herein, a missing native child elicits greater outrage than racist brutality against foreign innocents. Little provocation kindles prejudice and protest. Mental healthcare crumbles as youth suffer silently. And failure to nurture our young leaves them vulnerable to hidden threats.

This bleak portrait aims to spur reflection on how we reached such straits and what course corrections are required. The path ahead must be paved with expanded empathy, tolerance, and accountability.

Additionally, to any readers, I confirm none of the named personas relate to or reference any actual persons, living or deceased, except for our King and his Consort. Any such resemblances are wholly coincidental within the fictional framework.

I hope that thought-provoking stories like this can serve as cautionary tales to reinstate human decency before it becomes too late. Holding up a mirror to modern ills takes the first step towards righting them. If this work prompts a subtle rethinking of these themes, its intent has been fulfilled.

You may have noticed that the final documentary did not mention the tragic loss of life in the immigrant barge arson attack in Southampton. Nor were any details provided about the kidnapper's plans for Lucy.

While their focus remained squarely on updates surrounding Lucy's disappearance, the lack of attention to the plight of those impacted in the Southampton attack risks subtly dehumanising those victims through omission.

Additionally, some nuance was overlooked by prioritising their social media popularity over exploring what societal factors may have sparked such senseless violence.

These editorial choices illustrate how even well-intentioned journalism can sometimes inadvertently marginalise certain groups through selective focus. Moving forward, we must strive to cover all facets of a story with equal humanity and depth, not allowing anyone to become nameless or faceless, even inadvertently.

It is a tendency requiring constant vigilance.

Thank you for following this journey through an imagined yet conceivable descent into social disorder. Remember that redemption remains possible if we dare confront darkness with light.

As a final note, I wish to acknowledge this narrative was initially drafted in 2005, not as a commentary on current events in Britain, but rather relating to troubling circumstances facing the Romani community in Rome at that time, even if no kidnapping or rioting was involved.

The original story depicted the climate of prejudice and misguided backlash suffered by that marginalised group. It was adjusted to a modern London setting to underline how similar societal plights persist.

By reframing the fundamental themes around injustice and hostility toward misunderstood minority groups, I emphasised the timeless relevance of promoting tolerance regardless of the specific context.

While artistic liberties were taken to rework the backdrop to modern London, the core message highlighting and condemning undue suspicion cast on vulnerable populaces remains relevant across eras. If we do not learn from history, we will repeat it.

I appreciate your reading and hope this clarification provides a valuable perspective on the conceptual genesis of this timely yet timeless fictional work.

Godspeed!"

[The lights dim]

ACKNOWLEDGEMENT

First and foremost, I want to express my deepest gratitude to my family for their unwavering love and support through all of life's twists and turns. Mom, Dad, my two sisters - you are my foundation.

I owe immense thanks to my dear friend and mentor Carl Adamson. Without his sage advice and encouragement over the years, this book would not have been possible. And to his insightful wife Rosie, whose keen editorial eye and feedback on drafts was invaluable.

I also want to express my heartfelt appreciation to my friend Andrea Vestita, who provided incredibly insightful and illuminating feedback to this story, and not only, over the course of 30 years. I owe him a great debt for ensuring readers will be captivated by this story from beginning to end.

I'm grateful to the friends who read early versions and offered thoughtful perspectives as readers. Your enthusiasm kept me motivated. Any flaws that remain are my own.

Most of all, I want to thank the many people I've met during my life's journey so far who have shaped me into who I am. You know who you are, and how you've impacted my story. This book is a reflection of all your stories as well.

To everyone who accompanied me along the way - past, present and future - I could not have done this without you. My heartfelt appreciation for walking this path together.

Luigi Pascal

Printed in Great Britain
by Amazon

30196592R00078